George Denison Prentice, John James Piatt

The Poems of George D. Prentice

George Denison Prentice, John James Piatt

The Poems of George D. Prentice

ISBN/EAN: 9783337407735

Printed in Europe, USA, Canada, Australia, Japan

Cover: Foto ©Andreas Hilbeck / pixelio.de

More available books at **www.hansebooks.com**

THE POEMS

OF

GEORGE D. PRENTICE

EDITED

WITH A BIOGRAPHICAL SKETCH

BY JOHN JAMES PIATT

CINCINNATI

ROBERT CLARKE & CO

1876

DEDICATION.

———

CONTENTS.

BIOGRAPHICAL SKETCH.

GEORGE DENNISON PRENTICE was born upon a farm in the township of Preston, New London county, Connecticut, December 18, 1802. He was the second of two sons, the only children of his parents. His father, Rufus Prentice, was a man of fair average English education, and his mother, Sarah Stanton, is said to have had some literary culture and taste. George D. had reached manhood before his father's death, which took place in July, 1826; but his mother died during his boyhood, in November, 1816. An interesting and affecting record of her death may be found in his blank-verse poem, entitled " My Mother," printed in this volume. His tender and mournful regret for her is also indicated in the more familiar lines, "At my Mother's Grave," which, I believe, were writtten before he entered college. She taught him to read in the Bible at a very early age, and gave him religious impressions which, I know, lasted throughout his life. Mr. Prentice, one of whose earliest distinct recollections was of the total eclipse of the sun in 1806, as he once told me, remembered also to have read several chapters of the Bible on the day of that eclipse, when he was not quite three-and-a-half years old. His brother, fourteen months his senior, who is still living, relates that the neighbors visiting his father and mother, were in the habit of asking to hear George read, and that among them it was a common wonder so small a boy should read so well. Young Prentice's school experience began at a country school-house, before he had completed his fourth year; he showed remarkable precocity in mastering the common English branches. His father's means were small, it seems, and between his ninth and fourteenth years he was kept at work upon the farm— though somewhat delicate, doing a man's faithful service; but, his parents having meanwhile decided to give him a collegiate education, he was then placed under the instruction of a Presbyterian minister, previously a tutor at Yale, and in six months made such extraordinary progress in classical and other studies that he was fitted to enter any New England college of the time. During this marvelous half year, he began and completed the study of English grammar, having Lindley Murray by heart, within five days; he then, for the first time, took up a Latin grammar. In a biographical sketch (written by Mr. Henry Watterson, I believe, from an auto-biographic note left by Mr. Prentice) published in the Louisville Courier-Journal the morning after Mr. Prentice's death, is the following statement, referring to this period:

" He and two boys from South Carolina, one of them of his own age and the other two years older, were the clergyman's only pupils. His companions had each studied Latin two years, chiefly in their native State. They were in Virgil. In five weeks he caught up with the elder and more advanced, and the teacher, to save himself trouble, instructed the two to learn their lessons together, and recite them together. This was very annoying to young Prentice, for he found his comrade, the son of a wealthy planter, dull and slow. He remonstrated with his teacher, who, after a little burst of anger, gave him leave to go ahead in his own way. He went ahead. He recited the whole of the Twelfth Book of the Æneid, as a single half-day's lesson, to the Rev. Daniel Waldo, the uncle of his regular teacher, and extensively known, a few years ago, as the venerable Chaplain of Congress, who died, we believe, at the age of more than a hundred. He completed the study of Virgil, Horace, Sallust, Cicero's Orations, the Greek Testament, Xenophon, six books of Homer's Iliad, the Græca Minora, most of the Græca Majora, and other works, within six months after his first introduction to English grammar." But lacking the means necessary for beginning a college life, he now turned his attention to teaching, and, not yet fifteen, took charge of a village school, which he continued to teach for about two years. In the Autumn of 1820, he entered the Sophomore class at Brown University, where he so distinguished himself as a student, that Dr. Asa Messer, President of the College, pronounced him the best scholar who had ever been in the institution.   Here he exhibited the same remarkable power of memory manifested during his preparatory course of study ; it is stated, on Mr. Prentice's own authority, that he could recite *verbatim* the whole of Kames's " Elements of Criticism," Blair's " Rhetoric," and Dugald Stewart's " Mental Philosophy."   He became hardly less proficient in mathematics than in the ancient classics and modern literature.   Among his tutors at Brown were Horace Mann and Tristam Burges, both afterwards distinguished in different spheres of public life and action.   One of his college-mates was Dr. Samuel G. Howe, the well-known American philanthropist—and their early friendship continued throughout Mr. Prentice's life.

Having graduated, in 1823, Mr. Prentice taught in a seminary at Smithfield, for a time, in order to earn money sufficient for pursuing the study of law, which he began at Canterbury, and continued at Jewett, two Connecticut villages not far from his birth-place ; but after his admission to the bar, and perhaps a brief experience in the practice of law (not finding it to his taste, I dare say), he was drawn, partly by accident, into active journalism.   He had previously written somewhat for the press, I believe.   In 1827, on visiting his friend, John G. C. Brainard, the gentle poet of the Connecticut, at New London, he was persuaded to take charge of a local journal during its editor's two weeks' absence, and made such an impression in that time, that several offers were made to secure him as editor for various established or projected papers. He finally accepted the offer of two gentlemen who proposed to start a weekly paper at Hartford; he agreed to become its editor, and it was called The New England Review. Its first number was issued in the Autumn of 1828. It made at once a marked impression in New England, on account of both its political and literary character. It was the Louisville Journal, born in Connecticut. When its publication was begun, the opposing political parties in Connecticut had, in convention, nominated their Congressional tickets, the State being entitled to six Representatives. Not pleased with the candidates of his party, Mr. Prentice, upon his own responsibility, nominated the six men whom he thought best qualified, zealously urged their claims, and, in spite of vehement opposition, secured the election of all. This was very naturally regarded as a brilliant success.

In 1830, Mr. Prentice was induced by the Whigs of Connecticut to make a journey to Kentucky, for the purpose of visiting Ashland and preparing a life of Henry Clay. Meanwhile John G. Whittier, the poet, had been attracted, by the brightness, popular reputation and literary quality of The New England Review, to send some of his early poems as contributions to its columns; these had been published by Mr. Prentice, and so well liked by him that on leaving Hartford for Kentucky he recommended Mr. Whittier—then living at his father's house in Haverhill, Mass.—as a proper successor; and the latter was surprised one morning to receive a letter from the proprietors of The New England Review, asking his acceptance of the position. Mr. Whittier accepted it at once; but he had never met Mr. Prentice—they were strangers personally—and they did not afterwards meet each other, though Mr. Prentice, I know, always admired and honored the good Quaker poet of Amesbury, and the latter, I am sure, must always have remembered the generous compliment of Mr. Prentice.

The absence of Mr. Prentice from New England, when he came to Kentucky in 1830, was intended to be temporary; it was, so to speak, life-long. The biography of Henry Clay was designed simply for campaign uses in New England: it was written hastily from the standpoint of ardent partisanship, and it fulfilled its purpose; directly or indirectly, however, it served to make Mr. Prentice a citizen of Kentucky, for he had scarcely finished his task when he was persuaded, in connection with a gentleman from Ohio, to undertake the establishment of a new daily paper at Louisville, in opposition to the Jackson Democracy, who were purposing and planning to carry against Mr. Clay his own adopted State. Mr. Prentice's preface to the life of Henry Clay was dated November 14, 1830, and on the 24th of the same month the first number of the Louisville Journal appeared.

The newspaper of course at once became a warm political supporter of Mr. Clay, between whom and Mr. Prentice had begun an intimate personal friendship, which ended only with the former's death. The Louisville Journal soon began to attract attention, particularly by its peculiar short, sharp, epigrammatic paragraphs, which, as a general thing, flew to their mark like arrows—they were the winged words so often mentioned by Homer.

It seemed a hazardous thing for a stranger, and especially, perhaps, a " Yankee schoolmaster," as Mr. Prentice was called—on whom, I fancy, the Kentuckian in those old days was inclined to look, as Halleck pictures the Virginian doing,

> . . . . . . " with as favorable eyes
> As Gabriel on the devil in Paradise "—

to attempt such a style of editorial writing as Mr. Prentice adopted ; but he had the fearless courage—always mingled with generosity and good humor—necessary ; and, not shrinking from the ordeal, he went through it— making enemies often, but generally in the end making these enemies, if they were worthy ones, his friends. He and Shadrach Penn, an able writer, who, in 1830, was the recognized editorial champion of the Democratic party in Kentucky, conducting the Louisville Advertiser, fought bitterly in print for ten or twelve years, when the latter, who had been the aggressor, was compelled to leave the field of Kentucky journalism and emigrate to Missouri. But on the eve of his departure an interview was arranged between the two long hostile editors, by Dr. T. S. Bell, an eminent physician of Louisville, the friend of both, when Mr. Prentice cordially offered every influence in his power to render Mr. Penn's removal unnecessary; it being inevitable, he gave Mr. Penn his warm God-speed privately and in print. Mr. Penn established a new paper at St. Louis, but lived only four years afterwards, during which time he and Mr. Prentice remained personal friends. On Mr. Penn's death, his old editorial enemy wrote a very tender and generous eulogy of him. He did the same thing, much more recently, after the death of John H. Harney, for many years editor of the Louisville Democrat, between whom and Mr. Prentice a similar war of words was waged.

But paper bullets were not the only editorial missiles used in Kentucky. Mr. Prentice was never disposed to seek a personal·collision with anybody, but others were sometimes quick to attack him—not always, perhaps, without verbal aggravation, direct or indirect. Nearly all his personal encounters, I believe, ended with grace for himself. One particular affair of this kind is recorded, when a Kentucky editor named Trotter fired at Mr. Prentice on the street in Louisville, without warning, and wounded him near the heart. Mr. Prentice in a moment seized his assailant, threw him to the ground, and, with a knife given him by a spectator, in one hand, held him down with the other. "Kill him! kill him!" numbers of the crowd, which at once assembled, shouted. But Mr. Prentice instantly loosened his hold, saying, "I can not kill a disarmed and helpless man." Mr. Prentice was never, I believe, a party in any duel, and as early as 1854 he put on record his opinion of duelling so clearly and emphatically that I think it worth repeating. He had gone to Arkansas, to lend his influence toward some large railroad enterprise in that State, writing while there, for a Little Rock paper, articles in behalf of the scheme. One of these articles referred, somewhat pointedly, to arguments in opposition to the railroad enterprise published by a man named Hewson, who took offense at Mr. Prentice's expressions, and demanded their public withdrawal. Mr. Prentice answered that he was only criticising Hewson's writings, and disclaimed any intended imputation on his character or conduct. Hewson insisted on the unconditional withdrawal of the offensive expressions, intimating that otherwise Mr. Prentice would be expected to meet him in the field. Mr. Prentice repeated his disclaimer, adding:

"I do not recognize any right or reason, on your part, to ask or expect more of me. This I deem quite as much due to myself as to you.

"Presuming that your notes are written to me with a view to a duel, I may as well say here that I have not the least thought of accepting a challenge from you. I consider my strictures upon your writings entirely legitimate, and, at any rate, the disclaimer that I have made ought to satisfy you.

"I came here, from a distant State, because many believed I could do something to promote a great and important enterprise, and as I have reason to think that my labors are not altogether in vain, I do not intend to let myself be diverted from them. There are some persons, and perhaps many, to whom my life is valuable, and, however little or much value I may attach to it on my own account, I do not see fit, at present, to put it up voluntarily against yours.

"I am no believer in the duelling code. I would not call a man to the field unless he had done me such a deadly wrong that I desired to kill him, and I would not obey his call to the field unless I had done him so mortal an injury as to entitle him, in my opinion, to demand an opportunity of taking my life. I have not the least desire to kill you, or to harm a hair of your head, and I am not conscious of having done anything to entitle you to kill me. I do not want your blood upon my hands, and I do not want my own upon anybody's. I might yield much to the demands of a strong public sentiment, but there is no public sentiment, nor even any disinterested individual sentiment, that requires me to meet you, or would justify me in doing so.

"I look upon the miserable code, that is said to require two men to go out and shoot at each other for what one of them may consider a violation of etiquette or punctilio in the use of language, with a scorn equal to that which is getting to be felt for it by the whole civilized world of mankind. I am not afraid to express such views in the enlightened capital of Arkansas, or anywhere else. I am not so cowardly as to stand in dread of any imputation on my courage. I have always had courage enough to defend my honor and myself, and I presume I always shall have.

"Your most, etc.,   GEO. D. PRENTICE."

In the spring of 1835, Mr. Prentice married Miss Henrietta Benham, daughter of Joseph Benham, then a lawyer of some local distinction in Cincinnati and Louisville. Mrs. Prentice was a native of Ohio. She had great beauty of person in her youth, I have understood; in her middle life, when I first saw her, she was still fine-looking, having a handsome and attractive face, a stately figure, an elegant and gracious manner. With a naturally fine intellect, and many accomplishments of education, she had a heart of unusual sensibility—she could not listen without quick visible emotion to any tale of distress or suffering, and her charities near home were numerous. She enjoyed private distinction in Louisville as a singer, having a voice of much power and beauty, and showed talent as a composer of music. During her life the house of Mr. Prentice was a center of whatever was refined and graceful in Louisville society, Mrs. Prentice being for many years a social leader in that city. Mr. and Mrs. Prentice had in all four children, two of whom, a son and daughter, died in childhood; two sons, William Courtland and Clarence Joseph, lived until manhood.

I do not care to attempt any minute history of the Louisville Journal's long political career. In Mr. Prentice's hands it was always the most powerful and popular exponent of the Whig party in the South and West— indeed, for a time, it may be said, in the whole country.

It was for Mr. Prentice himself an engine of great personal force and influence. Doubtless, its greatest popularity and power were reached between 1840, the year of the great Whig triumph in Gen. Harrison's election to the Presidency, and 1860, when the war of the Southern Rebellion began. This period includes the Native American, or "Know Nothing" campaign, in which it was a zealous advocate of the Native American doctrine.

From the first, as I have said, the Louisville Journal attracted attention by its witty and epigrammatic paragraphs, and the most widely diffused reputation of Mr. Prentice, while living, was for the exhaustless wit and humor manifested day by day, for many years, in these. Only old men, or men now growing old, who were interested in the public affairs and persons of those days, and recall their atmosphere, know the wonderful vigor, effect, and currency of the paragraphs with which the Journal's columns bristled, as it were, from fifteen to forty-five years ago. They were copied and repeated far and wide. They went everywhere. London and Paris papers made frequent quotations of them. A volume containing selections from these paragraphs was published in 1859, entitled *Prenticeana* (the publisher's title), reprinted since Mr. Prentice's death. The volume was taken from the files of the Journal up to the date of publication. Mr. Prentice had long been urged to make such a collection, but had always declined, until at last it became evident that if he did not make it himself, others would attempt it, with far less regard for the feelings of men formerly his enemies, but then his friends, than he chose to exercise. When he finally compiled the volume, he carefully excluded, out of deference to the sensibilities of persons whom he had come to esteem and love, hundreds of the very passages which, at the time of their appearance, did most to give the Louisville Journal its fame, and suppressed very many of the names of individuals in the personal paragraphs retained. The copy originally prepared embraced perhaps thrice the matter printed in the book. This was submitted to two or three friends successively, with the request that each should suggest proper omissions, and the publishers were finally empowered, I believe, to reduce the collection to the requirements of the proposed volume; so, gradually, I am afraid, much of the best and most characteristic life passed out of the whole body of the book. Many of these paragraphs, however, removed from the day's columns, where they had the familiar atmosphere of the day about them, could hardly preserve the elusive something which had been their temporary "excuse for being." Mr. Prentice felt this when he wrote, in his modest preface: "I have no doubt that a very considerable portion of them, which, perhaps from partisan partiality, were deemed 'good hits' at the time, will, now that the occasion which called them forth has passed, be read with comparatively little interest. I know that such things do not keep well." Enough of them have kept well, however, to justify the reputation for abundant wit and humor which Mr. Prentice so long enjoyed—enough of them worthy to rank with the best good sayings which are quoted from Hook, and Lamb, and Sidney Smith, and Douglas Jerrold, or others of the famous wits of England. Let me venture to repeat a few, (but it is so easy to miss the best in such a collection, even when one thinks he finds them,) as I happen to turn to them in the volume :

"The editor of the ——— ' Statesman ' says more villany is on foot. We suppose the editor has lost his horse."

"James Ray and John Parr have started a locofoco paper in Maine, called the ' Democrat.' Parr, in all that pertains to decency, is below zero; and Ray is below Parr."

" ' Have I changed?' exclaims Gov. P——. We do n't know. That depends on whether you ever were an honest man."

" The [Washington] ' Globe ' says that such patriotism as Mr. Clay's will not answer. True enough, for it can't be questioned."

"The editor of the ——— speaks of his 'lying curled up in bed these cold mornings.' This verifies what we said of him some time ago—' he lies like a dog.'"

"The Philadelphia ' Ledger ' says that Clay, Calhoun, and Webster are behind the age. Then the age must be ' tail foremost.'"

"A young widow has established a pistol gallery in New Orleans. Her qualifications as a teacher of the art of dueling are of course undoubted; she has killed her man."

"Mr. William Hood was robbed near Corinth, Alabama, on the 13th inst. The Corinth paper says that the name of the highwayman is unknown, but there is no doubt that he was Robbin' Hood."

" A new Democratic paper in North Carolina is called 'The Rising Day.' It ought rather to be called the Night, for it is the shadow of the 'Globe.'"

" Mr. John Love, of Alabama, was recently lost during a passage from Texas to Mexico. We had supposed that no Love would ever be lost between those countries."

" The 'Globe' says that 'Mr. Clay is a sharp politician.' No doubt of it, but the editor of the 'Globe' is a sharper."

" Messrs. Bell and Topp, of the 'N. C. Gazette,' say that ''Prentices are made to serve masters.' Well, Bells were made to be hung, and Topps to be whipped."

Of a more general character, a few witticisms and epigrams may be given :

" Wild rye and wild wheat grow in some regions spontaneously. We believe that wild oats are always sown."

" Men are deserters in adversity; when the sun sets, and all is dark, our very shadows refuse to follow us."

" A well-known writer says that a fine coat covers a multitude of sins. It is still truer that such coats cover a multitude of sinners."

" When a man's heart ossifies, or turns to bone, he dies at once; but if it petrifies, or turns to stone, he invariably lives too long for any useful purpose."

" 'What would you do, madam, if you were a gentleman?' 'Sir, what would you do if you were one?'"

" Whatever Midas touched was turned into gold; in these days, touch a man with gold and he'll turn into anything."

" The botanists tell us that there is no such thing as a black flower. We suppose they never heard of the 'Coal-black Rose.'" [This was the heroine of an old-time negro song.]

" The man who lives only for this world is a fool here, and there is danger that he will be (we speak it not profanely) a d—d fool hereafter."

The Louisville Journal was never exclusively a political paper, although it was that chiefly. It gained, and for many years retained, a large literary reputation, especially as an avenue to the public for young poetical writers. If, as I have suggested, the New England Review was essentially the beginning of the Louisville Journal, then the name of Mr. Whittier, followed perhaps by that of Brainard, may head the long list of the Journal's occasional contributors, which included, later, the names of James Freeman Clarke, John Howard Payne, William D. Gallagher, Mrs. L. H. Sigourney, Mrs. Amelia Welby, Alice and Phœbe Cary, Mrs. C. A. Warfield, Mrs. Rosa Vertner Jeffrey, Fortunatus Cosby, William Ross Wallace, William W. Fosdick, William D. Howells, William Wallace Harney, Forceythe Willson, Elizabeth Conwell Smith (afterward Mrs. Willson), and others more or less known. I do not pretend to think greatly of all these writers, but this partial list contains several names sure of long life and honor in American literature. The late Forceythe Willson, for example, one of the most remarkable poets yet born in this country, first printed his peculiar verses in Mr. Prentice's paper. Many of his poems show somewhat of the eccentricity and strangeness found in the poetical writings of William Blake; but three or four of them, in their strong and noble sanity, pathetic power, dramatic realism, lofty and weird imagination, or tender beauty and delicacy of feeling, may safely be said to be far more valuable than all of Blake's best poetry, and hardly inferior to Edgar A. Poe's half-dozen leading productions. Several of Mrs. Welby's poems, which Mr. Prentice had originally published and commended, Poe himself highly praised, saying of her, in 1848: "Very few American poets are at all comparable with her in the true poetical qualities. As for our poetesses, . . few of them approach her." I do not think poets are produced by encouragement, but many a one already born has died and made no sign for lack of it, and—in America, where recognition of delicate and subtle genius in literature is slower than in other lands, although that of coarser and more vulgar strain is perhaps quicker and more instant than elsewhere—such a disposition as Mr. Prentice, in the midst of busy political engrossment, showed, and long continued to show, sole of American editors before or since, to encourage poetic manifestation, is memorable, and destined not to be soon forgotten in the history of American literature. As a specimen of his occasional private encouragement, I will quote from a letter written by him to a young girl, who, as he thought, exhibited unmistakeable genius of high order, and for whom he always cherished, until his death, the sincerest and highest regard. A friend had shown him some of her girlish verses, which he had published, and he had already written to her more briefly concerning them. It will be observed that his confident prophecy is well guarded by wise conditions, and his criticism and advice are no less wise than gentle :

> *"Dec.* 25, [1855.]

"I am glad that my brief letter was gratifying to you. Having heard that you are a little cynical, I did not know how you would receive it. But, thinking that you perhaps needed, and knowing that you deserved, encouragement, I resolved to express to you my appreciation of your genius. And I now say emphatically to you again, as I believe I said to you then, that, if you are entirely true to yourself, and if your life be spared, you will, in the maturity of your powers, be the first poet of your sex in the United States. I say this, not as what I think, but as what I know.

. . . "It was far from my design to suggest to you not to write poetry in your hours of sadness. We must all have hours of mournful feeling, and probably it is the case with most poets that their somber and melancholy thoughts and reflections are more essentially poetical than their joyous ones. I would have you utter all the poetical thoughts that arise in your soul except the morbid and misanthropic ones A tender sorrow is as healthful as joy, and as beautiful. Strike all that is sad from the works of our greatest poets, and their fame would be more than half destroyed.

> 'Who would be doomed to look upon
> A sky without a cloud ? '

. . . "I have no doubt that your mind, as you intimate, has felt the unhealthful influences of the pages of Byron. I have, like yourself, an almost boundless admiration for the genius of that extraordinary man, but I do believe that it would have been better for mankind if he had never lived. I think that he made his mighty gifts a curse to the world. It is unfortunate that greatness ever exists without goodness—that there should ever be a great soul that neither loves man nor worships God. The glitter of the genius of an unhallowed nature is like the flashes of the lightning on a rock-bound coast, revealing only wreck and desolation. Read Byron, if you will, but do not yield yourself up to the fascinations of the deadly serpent that coils among the beautiful and glorious flowers upon his page.

"The nerves of my fingers are so diseased that I usually do all my writing by an amanuensis. This is the longest letter that I have written with my own hand for fifteen years. I hope you will write to me.   Your friend,

"Geo. D. Prentice."

The allusion in the closing paragraph was to a paralysis in his writing fingers, (a disease known professionally, I believe, as *chorea scriptorum*,) which, during the last twenty-five years of his life, made dictation to an amanuensis necessary for the great mass of his editorial writing. By painful exertion, however, he often wrote paragraphs and brief notes with his own hand. At one time he learned to use the pen in his left hand, and at another he tried a writing-machine. The letter from which I have quoted, like many later ones in my possession, appears in his own neat, delicate, and always carefully punctuated and legible manuscript.

During his lifetime the reputation which Mr. Prentice enjoyed for his own poetry was hardly less than that which his wit and humor gave him. I have already said that the lines entitled "At my Mother's Grave," which have been highly praised for their melodious tenderness and mournful beauty of feeling, were written, while their author was yet in his boyhood, before he entered college. Mr. Prentice certainly began his career as a poet, but, like

William Cullen Bryant, he made journalism the business of his life. I doubt if Mr. Bryant has ever given himself up so entirely to his public profession as did Mr. Prentice. The latter, as an editor, was always a great worker—rising early (as I remember him in some of the closing years of his life) and going to his editorial table, while merchants' clerks were yet at breakfast; then sitting, with brief intervals, throughout the day, and often until late at night, devoting himself to his endless task-work. But all along, from youth to the approach of old age, he retained his early freshness of feeling and appetite for poetry, and continued to write it. Although he produced his most distinctive and popular poems while young, many of his later pieces seem hardly inferior to his best early ones.

I am disposed to think there is no other American poet, except Mr. Bryant, who has so finely handled blank verse as Mr. Prentice has done in several of his principal poems. His blank verse, indeed, occasionally suggests a resemblance to that of Mr. Bryant, although much more of emotional element and warmth of color— the visible life of human passion—are noticeable in it. He lacked that careful eye for the little half-secrets of Nature shown by Mr. Bryant, but his real love of Nature was no less true. Born in the country, he never lost its early influence in the dust and heat of the city, as one may clearly read in the fragments (which I have found only under distinct heads, but have placed together under one) entitled "My Old Home." In nearly all of Mr. Prentice's more serious poetry—especially in his blank-verse poems—the current of feeling is in sympathy with the great works of Nature; we find frequent allusions to the stars, the ocean, mountains, clouds, winds, storms, and rainbows—to the beautiful and wonderful facts and phenomena of earth and sky.

If "Thanatopsis" is Mr. Bryant's representative poem in blank verse, "The Closing Year" may be said to be that of Mr. Prentice—it has long been so at least in popular regard. I do not know where there may be found a more stately and solemn meditation on the flight of Time, and the changes wrought thereby, than this poem presents; and I doubt if in English poetry there exists a more striking or loftier personification of Time, and allusion to his conquests, than its concluding lines afford. One of Mr. Prentice's faults in this, as in many other of his pieces, is an overstrong tendency to rhetorical movement and effect. "The River in the Mammoth Cave" is freer from this fault, though it has in one of its lines another fault, too frequent in Mr. Prentice's poetry —unhappy use of metaphor. He is speaking of the various formations in the great cavern resembling flowers,

"Carved by the magic *fingers* of the *drops*."

But this poem seems to me one of his best, and I prefer it to "The Closing Year:" it has a peculiar somberness of quiet feeling—its current of sentiment is as mournfully toned as the weird river it celebrates. "The Mammoth Cave" is more cheerful in its teaching, but is hardly less striking.

Among others of Mr. Prentice's poems in blank verse may be mentioned the piece entitled "My Mother," which is in parts very tender and touching, with great beauty of expression, and indicates the strong hold his mother's memory had upon his heart during his busy, striving, and stormy manhood. I think it hardly inferior to Cowper's lines referring to his mother's picture—the experience given in them, the remembrance of a mother's death in early boyhood, is similar. "The Grave of the Beautiful" is touched with lovely and delicate hues of feeling, as is also "The Invalid's Reply." The last-named has passages of exquisite beauty and tenderness. "Lookout Mountain," "Thoughts on the Far Past," and "On the Summit of the Sierra Madre" are among the latest poems in blank verse by Mr. Prentice. They were all written during the last ten years of his life. The first of the three pieces just mentioned realizes with much vigor the desperate fight described—the battle above the clouds; and each of them has passages of fine quality, which it would be difficult to surpass with quotation from recent American or English blank verse.

Among his many poems in rhyme, the verses "To an

Absent Wife,"—written, while Mr. Prentice was visiting a water-cure establishment on the Gulf of Mexico, many years ago, in ill health—have been deservedly popular; the last stanza is particularly terse and beautiful :

> "I sink in dreams :—low, sweet, and clear,
> Thy own dear voice is in my ear;
> Around my neck thy tresses twine;
> Thy own loved hand is clasped in mine;
> Thy own soft lip to mine is pressed;
> Thy head is pillowed on my breast :—
> Oh! I have all my heart holds dear,
> And I am happy—thou art here!"

Of other pieces tender in sentiment, but referring to more youthful experience—and written in his youth—there are several, of which the one entitled "Memories" is perhaps the most pleasing.

Mr. Prentice wrote many poems merely sentimental, without any real root in the heart; and not a few of these, some of which are included in this volume, are commonplace; too many of them contain identical allusions and figures—indeed, he had an easy disposition to repeat himself, especially in the many pieces which he addressed to persons.   But several of his sentimental poems are very delicately finished—" To a Bunch of Roses," and "Lines to a Lady," for example.   The first named, particularly, is exquisite, and both show the poet's terseness and epigrammatic felicity of expression.   Two or three pieces of still lighter quality may be mentioned as good specimens of *vers de societe*—" The Bouquet's Compliments," "Fanny," and "To the Daughter of an Old Sweetheart."

Mr. Prentice was always modest regarding his poetic gift, as he was indeed modest regarding all his gifts. I remember to have heard him say, soon after I first knew him, that he did not think himself entitled to the name of poet, for which he had an exalted respect. Yet from first to last, something of the poetic distinction was always observable even in his more serious prose, which has here and there poetic color and cadence—and indeed it shows itself occasionally in his volume of paragraphs. He was often persuaded to publish his poems in book form, many years before his death, but always declined, preferring they should only appear in this shape after that event.

It must not be supposed that Mr. Prentice's editorial writing was confined to his myriad brief paragraphs. These were but the quick skirmishers of his moving and active force. He wrote long and earnest, often eloquent and powerful, leading articles, throughout his editorial career, on all themes of large general or political interest. Having great fertility of resources, he would sometimes produce, in a single day, matter enough for use in several successive numbers of the Journal. Besides doing this work addressed directly to the public, and besides writing his poems, he was always a frequent letter-writer. Knowing intimately most of the leading public men of his day—statesmen, politicians, editors, military men, artists, and authors—they were his occasional correspondents. He wrote numerous letters to ladies—very many of whom, distinguished in literature or society, were his acquaintances and friends; I dare say that his best and most characteristic letters were of the latter class. From a number which lie before me, I will copy three or four, in whole or part, to show the quality of his epistolary writing; in doing so I shall incidentally illustrate the gentler social and domestic side of his character. These letters are full of familiar gossip, playful wit, and humorous pleasantry. His correspondent was the same young lady to whom a letter already quoted was addressed two or three years earlier. Between her and the ladies of his household—which, besides Mrs. Prentice, included his brother's daughter and the sister of his most valued and confidential editorial associate—there was a friendly intimacy, and she had recently visited them :

"*Oct.* 21, [1858.]

" Mrs. Prentice and the young ladies are delighted to hear from you, and all send you their love. Mr. B—— is now one of us, and I trust that he will not soon leave us. His genial feelings, his quiet wit, his gentle manners, and his keen appreciation of the beautiful and the good make him a very charming companion. But I believe I need not praise him to you.

   ※   ※   ※   ※   ※   ※   ※

"We have had some good laughs about your Memphis admirer, who, I believe, is really a very clever fellow. A couple of days after you left here, he addressed a formal note to H——, informing her, in words ominous of a solemn intent, that he wished to call and see her at a particular hour. He made the call, and afterward came to me and asked my consent to let him invite her to the theater. He got my consent, but failed to get hers, and she has not seen him since. So she will not be at all in your way."

The illness mentioned in the following letter was an erysipelas which attacked Mr. Prentice in his face, and confined him to a darkened room for several weeks. The mock-earnest allusion to young men and women playing at cross-purposes in love is charming, and very characteristic; it recalls that little poem of Moschus, which Shelley has translated, beginning:

" Pan loved his neighbor, Echo—but that child," etc.

                                        "*Nov.* 13, [1858.]
"I have been hoping all along to be able to come to N—— for M—— S—— to-day, but I am disappointed. Her brother goes for her, and I send by him this little missive of memory and affection.

"I was out of my prison for a little while three or four days ago, but I am back in it now, without any strong hope of a speedy release. My patience, which was considerable, is utterly exhausted, and I almost wish to die. I requested my barber, when he visited me this morning, to cut my throat for me; but he declined doing it, and somehow I do n't altogether like to do it myself. Not unfrequently, however, I find myself repeating, with vehement gesture, the soliloquy of the Danish gentleman who saw his father's ghost, 'To be or not to be—that is the question.'

"I had engagements abroad for the present month, which would have been worth nearly —— thousand dollars to me, but I have had to abandon them all. This poor, pitiful malady, which has not even the dignity of being dangerous, has compelled me to give them up, and may force me to give up those of December and January. I do not know of any one who guards his health more vigilantly than I do mine, and certainly I know of no one whose vigilance is more indifferently rewarded. 'T is very hard, but, I suppose, perfectly right. This sounds very much like resignation—does n't it? But I am *not* resigned, and I *can not* be.

"Mr. S—— will tell you that we are all well except myself. We all retain a sweet memory of your visit, and cherish the hope that you will ere long come to us again. Mr. B—— has been getting ready to paint portraits, and expects to be able to open his room on Monday. I regret deeply that I can not be out, for I should be able to bring him at once as much work as he can do. I have no doubt, however, that, even if I have to lie here, he will do well, for he is a fine artist, and has a great many admirers and friends. You seem to have objected to his addressing a piece of poetry to '——' [a pseudonym]. Ah, you were a little jealous, I suppose. However, you need n't have been, for you perhaps saw, from a subsequent number of the ——, that, although he was in love with '——,' there was no chance of a match in the case, inasmuch as '——' is desperately in love with *me*. How young men and women do play at cross-purposes. Here's poor Mr. B. in love with '——' and poor '——' in love with me, and poor I in love with you, and poor you in love with somebody else, or rather a dozen somebody elses. The Lord pity us!

"I had a letter from A—— yesterday, and have had three or four from her quite recently. She tells me that she has just written to you, and uses many words of love and endearment in speaking of you. . . . She is a young girl with many of a young girl's weaknesses, but, in view of her genius, I almost feel toward her, whether absent from her or present with her, the awe that a glorious young prophetess would inspire. . . .

"Won't you send me a few lines by M—— S——? Do, for

your words will come like sweet tones of music into my sad room. . . . . Devotedly your friend,

"Geo. D. Prentice."

In this next letter the writer has recovered from his illness, and makes humorous allusion to its nature. The letter is full of gayety and brightness; Mr. Prentice's wit and humor show themselves at genial play throughout. In each of these quoted letters, since I present them only as specimens of his writing, I have removed the real names, or veiled them under initials:

"*Nov.* 20, [1858.]

"I am out of my sick room at last, and looking handsomer than you ever saw me in your life. It seems I did not bear my malady with as much fortitude as you would have expected of me. Well, I acknowledge that fortitude and patience did give way. I could have borne the pain well enough, and, if the malady had been dangerous, I suppose I could have stood that tolerably well for a sinner, but then, you see, the foul fiend attacked my *beauty*, and, even if I had been as good a Christian as you are, I should no doubt have murmured and grumbled at that.

"You complain that I do not answer your questions. Well, I will, so far as I can remember them, though I do n't think you always mean much by them. I think that Mr. ——, of Memphis, was really inconsolable. He did not go off at the time he had intended, nor for ten days afterward, although he had no business here. Several times, when H—— was shopping, he walked back and forth on the opposite side of the street, to obtain the small comfort of a look at her, though he never ventured to call upon her after his repulse. Byron says that

. . . 'There is nothing so consoles a man
As rum and true religion,'

and, as Mr. —— does not enjoy the consolations of religion, I rather think he betook himself slightly to rum.

"I have not seen Gov. M—— since you left us. I have had two letters from him, and in each of them he talks about R——, but says not a word about you. Hang him! he has no taste, and I will never support him again for Governor or anything else—unless, indeed, R—— bids me do it; for you know I could refuse nothing to her. Judge ——, until your visit here, was a most indefatigable beau, but I have not heard of his visit to a lady since. He looks very melancholy, and sighs like a bellows—pining himself to death, I fear, for that pretty curl of yours. He thought the curl troublesome to you, but it has no doubt been a thousand times more troublesome to him—poor fellow! I learn that three or four prisoners have been sent to the penitentiary simply from his absence of mind or inattention to his duties upon the bench; and I think you ought to ask Gov. M—— for their pardon, or rather to persuade R—— to do so. What say you?

"We often talk of you in our family as familiarly and affectionately as if you belonged to it—and I wish to Heaven you did. You ask why Mr. ——, while all the rest send love to you, never sends even his compliments. I think the reason must be—first that he is very far from being a 'demonstrative' young gentleman, and secondly, that he probably never knows when I am going to write to you. He certainly admires your genius very much. He was the first person that ever mentioned you to me. On his return from N——, about three years ago, he exclaimed to me, with as near an approach to enthusiasm as he ever makes, 'I have discovered a new poet.'

❋   ❋   ❋   ❋   ❋   ❋   ❋

"M—— S—— will probably write you to-day, and I believe she has redeemed her promise in regard to Z——. Mr. B—— thinks your poem to him [a pleasantry of make-believe sentiment, written in company with the young ladies of Mr. Prentice's household, which accidentally got into print,] the sweetest thing in the world, and I suppose he will attempt a retort, of course. You have probably observed that, in his poetry, he has recently been going into the love-making line pretty extensively. I never write love poetry to the ladies now. If I let them write it to me, I think 't is quite as much as they can reasonably expect."

Of more serious expressions than are found in the foregoing, not a few quotations might be made. Here is one in which Mr. Prentice refers to his religious faith—the letter from which it is taken, though addressed to the same person, was written a year or two before those last quoted :

"I rejoice, my little friend, that you are a believer. For my own part, I have no doubt either of the truths of Christianity, or of the momentous and infinite importance of those truths. I hear a thousand things from the pulpit that make me smile, yet I would rather be a Christian of the very humblest order of intellect than the most gloriously-gifted infidel that ever blazed like a comet through the atmosphere of earth."

And here is an earnest and eloquent passage concerning "the fame that men hunt after in their lives," with which I may fitly close my quotations, and return to the current of Mr. Prentice's life :

"I think, my young friend, that you mean to be a little satirical when you allude to what I said about your ability to win a fame that might shine like a star above your tomb. The figure may not be a happy one, but I am sure there is in your heart, as in all high hearts, a craving to be remembered among men. There is a mighty hunger of the soul, which only the dream of fame can appease. . . . You may call fame an '*ignis fatuus*,' but the greatest of the sons of men have worshiped, and will ever worship it, as devoutly as the Persian bowed to the eternal fires of the sky."

During several years immediately preceding the Southern Rebellion, Mr. Prentice appeared at seasons as a public lecturer, delivering two or three discourses on national politics in many of the Northern and Southern cities. One of his lectures had for its theme the American Statesmanship of the day. In this he presented a gloomy outlook at the future of the country. A life-long admirer and friend of Henry Clay, he lamented the latter's comparatively recent departure:— "Ulysses," he said, "has gone upon his wandering, and there is none left in all Ithaca to bend his bow." He predicted wide public misfortune, and his dark prophecies were criticised as morbidly melancholy; but the result proved their groundwork of truth. The Southern secession movement was already brooding, and soon the storm fell. Mr. Prentice opposed the Southern movement earnestly, in private conversation and in print, from the first. He had no doubt, he often said, of the result of the civil war which he thought would certainly follow the election of Abraham Lincoln, and the consequent secession of the South; but the Bell and Everett party—the temporary Conservative Union party, which he warmly supported—having failed, he recognized no other course but to accept, and, if necessary, support the Republican Union administration of Lincoln.

Strong efforts were made by the Southern leaders to

secure the Journal's powerful influence in behalf of the Confederacy ; but, although one or two of his business associates were not indisposed to accept the overtures, Mr. Prentice persistently turned his face away. Afterward, I remember, he told me that he might have become very wealthy if he had joined the fortunes of the Rebellion. The importance of keeping the Louisville Journal as an active support of the Union cause in Kentucky, was recognized at the national capital, and its large immediate loss of Southern patronage was in part compensated by the Federal government. Mr. Prentice visited Washington several times during the years 1861 and 1862, and was always treated with distinction by the President and his cabinet. President Lincoln, who had been an early reader and admirer of the Louisville Journal, held its editor in high esteem, and, during the early months of Mr. Lincoln's administration, Mr. Prentice had strong personal influence with him. At a dinner given to Mr. Prentice, in Washington, early in 1862, by a prominent Republican official, various members of the cabinet being present, he was toasted by the Secretary of War as having himself charge of the War Department in Kentucky. The Louisville Journal was largely instrumental in keeping Kentucky within the Union.

Mr. Prentice's course, however, though it was his path of duty, was a painful one. Both of his sons were eagerly Southern in feeling, each having been educated in part at Southern military schools. The younger, Clarence, could not be restrained from joining the Confederate army at the start. Mr. Prentice's elder son, Courtland, who had been persuaded to remain upon a farm which his father had given him, near Louisville, during the early months of the Rebellion, left it—much to his father's regret and disappointment—in September, 1862, and entered a company belonging to Morgan's cavalry. Mrs. Prentice, I believe, sent her heart with her boys, sympathizing with the cause they had adopted. Less than a month after Courtland joined the Confederate army, his dead body was brought home for burial. He was killed in battle, at Augusta, Ky. Mr. Prentice loved his sons warmly, and the death of this one gave him great sorrow. He wrote to me a few weeks later, saying: "I am grateful to you for your sympathy. I need it, and I need God's pity. I feel very, very desolate. The wind of death has swept over my life and left it a desert, but in my sadness I will try to do my duty." And, again, somewhat later, he said: "I am in bad spirits, my dear friend, for my own sake and our country's. My son is dead, and sometimes I almost fear that my country, too, may perish. I see no palm-tree upon the desert which surrounds me." His younger son's early connection with the Rebellion did not seem to have grieved him so much. Although he was devotedly attached to both his sons, the elder seemed to be his favorite.

Meanwhile, during the few days of Courtland's military life in an invading army, (for this was during the Confederate occupation of Kentucky,) Mr. Prentice himself—in a city where his dearest friends by hundreds were Confederates—was one of the easily-counted tens willing to shoulder his gun as a volunteer home-guard, to protect that city from the same invading army. Long afterward, he told me—as something which then struck him humorously—of a midnight alarm, during this brief period of his volunteer service, when it was supposed the enemy was advancing upon the city; the bells were rung, a premeditated signal, and out of hundreds who came to the rendezvous, there were but about sixty besides himself to go into the ranks for instant duty. The alarm, however, proved a false one.

At the return of peace Mr. Prentice was an old man, and the days of his popularity and power were gone. Mrs. Prentice died in April, 1868. After her death he lived for a time with his son Clarence—who had continued in the Confederate service, gaining the rank of a Colonel, until the close of the Rebellion—at his old home in Louisville; but, Clarence having exchanged the city property, which had been given him by his parents, for a farm several miles out of town, Mr.

Prentice, during the remainder of his life, occupied a small room at the Journal (then recently become the Courier-Journal) office—working, eating, sleeping there, and, since he was in ill health and feeble much of the time, seldom going out. Though the control of the newspaper had passed into other hands, he still worked steadfastly on in the old way. He had suffered occasionally for many years from a heart disease, which afflicted him seriously during the last year of his life, and it would hardly have been strange if he had been found dead some morning at his writing-table. But, a day or two before Christmas, 1869, he started from Louisville, during a season of bitter winter weather, to visit the farm of his son, and, riding in an open carriage, contracted a severe cold, which, developing into pneumonia, was the direct cause of his death. He died on the morning of January 22, 1870. A lady who was present during his last moments asked me subsequently: "What do you suppose Mr. Prentice meant in his last expressions? Just before his death he seemed to arouse himself and said—we heard him distinctly—'I want an *o*;' and then, again, 'I want an *i*.' We at first supposed he said, 'I want to go,' and these were reported to have been his last words; but I have often thought of these expressions, and wondered what could have been their meaning." Knowing Mr. Prentice's long habit of dictation in writing, and his manner of correcting his manuscript, which he always seemed carefully to overlook while walking to and fro, or sitting at the table opposite his amanuensis, it occurred to me that he may have been at the time in a slight delirium, and supposed himself dictating an article. I think this explanation was perhaps a just one, and that the tireless old editor died in a dream of correcting his copy. Yet he had always kept in sight his early religious education, and I know that he anticipated his death, and, I believe, did not dread it.

In person Mr. Prentice was slightly above the medium stature, with a figure, when in vigorous health, inclined to stoutness. His features were not regular, but his face was for the most part pleasing; often, when animated, it seemed handsome. His head was finely shaped, having a particularly noble and impressive forehead. His hair was black, but somewhat thin—retaining its blackness until quite late in his life. He had dark-brown eyes, rather small, full of light and sparkle when he was in a happy mood, though they could express fierceness and severity. The engraved likeness of him in this volume is from a daguerreotype taken about the year 1856 or 1857, when he was between fifty-four and fifty-five years old. It represents him at his best, as I remember him. His voice was low and agreeable in its general tone. Among strangers he was apt to be reserved, sometimes embarrassed; but with chosen friends his convertion was fluent and free—often full of characteristic brightness and humor; at other times—when touching the loftier themes of poetry and philosophy—seriously sweet and eloquent.

The leading traits of Mr. Prentice's character have been illustrated, I believe, in the facts of his life and the quotations from his writings which I have given. A man of the true *genus irritabile*, he was quickly impulsive, but his impulses were full of generosity. One of his friends once said of him to me: " He has the largest heart that ever beat." Mr. G. W. Griffin, who published a sketch of Mr. Prentice's life some years ago, relates, on the authority of Fortunatus Cosby, the poet, an anecdote which gives happy emphasis to what I have said of his generosity of impulse. A man named —— who had started certain scandalous reports concerning Mr. Prentice, which the latter had not troubled himself to notice, had the boldness to call upon him at his office several years afterward, with outworn, unclean garments, and in a repulsive personal condition. Mr. Cosby being present, —— called Mr. Prentice aside, and, after a little conversation, left the room. Mr. Cosby, a familiar friend of Mr. Prentice, asked the name of his unsightly visitor. " He is Thomas Jefferson ——. He told me he was in distress, and that he wanted two dollars and a half, for the purpose of going to see his mother." "Yes," answered Mr. Cosby, " and I suppose you were silly enough to give it to him?" "No," replied Mr. Prentice; "I recollected that I had a mother, and asked myself the question, what she would have thought of me had I appeared before her in such a condition. I gave him twenty-five dollars, and told him to go and see his mother in the dress of a gentleman." Thousands of dollars were given away, first and last, by Mr. Prentice in a similar manner, to needy young men passing through Louisville. Mr. Prentice was a warm and steadfast friend, and a noble enemy. That he was not without faults I need not deny. One of his chief faults, as he once confessed to me pleasantly, was a life-long inabilty to say "No" with sufficient distinctness. But whatever his faults may have been, he was always cordial in acknowledging the virtues of others.

Upon the death of Mr. Prentice, great immediate respect was shown to his memory in Louisville, and throughout the country. The Legislatures of Kentucky and Tennessee, then in session, each passed resolutions calling his death a public grief. The Kentucky Legislature invited Mr. Henry Watterson, the friend and associate of his latter years, to prepare and deliver an address before it on Mr. Prentice's career and character:—this Mr. Watterson did very ably, a few days later.

Mr. Prentice was a Mason, and his body, removed from his son's house to Louisville, was permitted to lie in state during one day in the Masonic Temple, where thousands of his fellow-citizens—men, women, and children—thronged to take their last look at his familiar face. He was buried with Masonic honors in Cave Hill Cemetery, by the side of his wife and near the graves of his children.. No monument at present marks his grave, unless a rose-bush which stands at his head be one. Once, when I visited it, several years ago, a violet, planted by some tender hand, was growing above the poet's breast, recalling his early lines on his mother's grave :

> " The violet, with its blossoms blue and mild,
> Waves o'er thy head; when shall it wave
> Above thy child?"

But there is in course of execution, at Louisville, a statue, considerably larger than life-size, in Carrara marble, representing Mr. Prentice sitting in his editorial chair in an accustomed meditative attitude, which is destined to stand, supported by granite pillars, at an elevation of nearly forty feet, in front of the new Courier-Journal building, adjoining the Public Library of Kentucky, and look down upon the busy street which so long knew and honored Mr. Prentice in life. This will be a fitting local monument of him in his public capacity as an editor, statesman, and patriot; but a book is not confined to a city, and I believe there is something in this volume of his poems, which, although it may not be a moving and active force in the busy world, will survive the marble effigy in the memory of men.

POEMS

OF

GEORGE D. PRENTICE.

THE CLOSING YEAR.

'TIS midnight's holy hour—and silence now
   Is brooding, like a gentle spirit, o'er
The still and pulseless world.　Hark! on the winds
The bell's deep notes are swelling.　'T is the knell
Of the departed Year.
                  No funeral train
Is sweeping past; yet on the stream and wood,
With melancholy light, the moonbeams rest,
Like a pale, spotless shroud; the air is stirred,
As by a mourner's sigh; and on yon cloud,
That floats so still and placidly through heaven,
The spirits of the seasons seem to stand—
Young Spring, bright Summer, Autumn's solemn form,
And Winter with his aged locks—and breathe
In mournful cadences, that come abroad
Like the far wind-harp's wild and touching wail,
A melancholy dirge o'er the dead Year,
Gone from the earth forever.
                    'T is a time
For memory and for tears.　Within the deep,
Still chambers of the heart, a specter dim,

Whose tones are like the wizard voice of Time,
Heard from the tomb of ages, points its cold
And solemn finger to the beautiful
And holy visions that have passed away
And left no shadow of their loveliness
On the dead waste of life.   That specter lifts
The coffin-lid of hope, and joy, and love,
And, bending mournfully above the pale
Sweet forms that slumber there, scatters dead flowers
O'er what has passed to nothingness.
                              The Year
Has gone, and, with it, many a glorious throng
Of happy dreams.   Its mark is on each brow,
Its shadow in each heart.   In its swift course,
It waved its scepter o'er the beautiful,
And they are not.   It laid its pallid hand
Upon the strong man, and the haughty form
Is fallen, and the flashing eye is dim.
It trod the hall of revelry, where thronged
The bright and joyous, and the tearful wail
Of stricken ones is heard, where erst the song
And reckless shout resounded   It passed o'er
The battle-plain, where sword and spear and shield
Flashed in the light of midday—and the strength
Of serried hosts is shivered, and the grass,
Green from the soil of carnage, waves above
The crushed and mouldering skeleton.   It came

And faded like a wreath of mist at eve ;
Yet, ere it melted in the viewless air,
It heralded its millions to their home
In the dim land of dreams.

                         Remorseless Time !—
Fierce spirit of the glass and scythe !—what power
Can stay him in his silent course, or melt
His iron heart to pity ? On, still on
He presses, and forever. The proud bird,
The condor of the Andes, that can soar
Through heaven's unfathomable depths, or brave
The fury of the northern hurricane
And bathe his plumage in the thunder's home,
Furls his broad wings at nightfall, and sinks down
To rest upon his mountain-crag—but Time
Knows not the weight of sleep or weariness,
And night's deep darkness has no chain to bind
His rushing pinion. Revolutions sweep
O'er earth, like troubled visions o'er the breast
Of dreaming sorrow ; cities rise and sink,
Like bubbles on the water ; fiery isles
Spring, blazing, from the ocean, and go back
To their mysterious caverns ; mountains rear
To heaven their bald and blackened cliffs, and bow
Their tall heads to the plain ; new empires rise,
Gathering the strength of hoary centuries,
And rush down like the Alpine avalanche,

Startling the nations; and the very stars,
Yon bright and burning blazonry of God,
Glitter awhile in their eternal depths,
And, like the Pleiad, loveliest of their train,
Shoot from their glorious spheres, and pass away,
To darkle in the trackless void: yet Time,
Time the tomb-builder, holds his fierce career,
Dark, stern, all-pitiless, and pauses not
Amid the mighty wrecks that strew his path,
To sit and muse, like other conquerors,
Upon the fearful ruin he has wrought.

AT MY MOTHER'S GRAVE.

THE trembling dew-drops fall
   Upon the shutting flowers; like souls at rest,
The stars shine gloriously: and all,
     Save me, are blest.

   Mother, I love thy grave!
The violet, with its blossoms blue and mild,
    Waves o'er thy head; when shall it wave
      Above thy child?

   'Tis a sweet flower, yet must
Its bright leaves to the coming tempest bow;
    Dear mother, 'tis thine emblem—dust
      Is on thy brow.

   And I could love to die:
To leave untasted life's dark, bitter streams—
    By thee, as erst in childhood, lie,
      And share thy dreams.

   And must I linger here,
To stain the plumage of my sinless years,
    And mourn the hopes to childhood dear
      With bitter tears?

Aye, must I linger here,
A lonely branch upon a withered tree,
Whose last frail leaf, untimely sere,
Went down with thee?

Oft from life's withered bower,
In still communion with the Past, I turn,
And muse on thee, the only flower
In Memory's urn.

And, when the evening pale
Bows, like a mourner, on the dim blue wave,
I stray to hear the night-winds wail
Around thy grave.

Where is thy spirit flown?
I gaze above—thy look is imaged there;
I listen—and thy gentle tone
Is on the air.

Oh, come, while here I press
My brow upon thy grave; and, in those mild
And thrilling tones of tenderness,
Bless, bless thy child!

Yes, bless thy weeping child;
And o'er thine urn—Religion's holiest shrine—
Oh, give his spirit, undefiled,
To blend with thine.

THE RIVER IN THE MAMMOTH CAVE.

OH, dark, mysterious stream, I sit by thee
    In awe profound, as myriad wanderers
Have sat before. I see thy waters move
From out the ghostly glimmerings of my lamp
Into the dark beyond, as noiselessly
As if thou wert a somber river drawn
Upon a spectral canvas, or the stream
Of dim Oblivion flowing through the lone
And shadowy vale of death. There is no wave
To whisper on thy shore, or breathe a wail,
Wounding its tender bosom on thy sharp
And jagged rocks. Innumerous mingled tones,
The voices of the day and of the night,
Are ever heard through all our outer world,
For Nature there is never dumb ; but here
I turn and turn my listening ear, and catch
No mortal sound, save that of my own heart,
That 'mid the awful stillness throbs aloud,
Like the far sea-surf's low and measured beat
Upon its rocky shore. But when a cry,
Or shout, or song is raised, how wildly back

Come the weird echoes from a thousand rocks,
As if unnumbered airy sentinels,
The genii of the spot, caught up the voice,
Repeating it in wonder—a wild maze
Of spirit-tones, a wilderness of sounds,
Earth-born but all unearthly.

      Thou dost seem,
O wizard stream, a river of the dead—
A river of some blasted, perished world,
Wandering forever in the mystic void.
No breeze e'er strays across thy solemn tide ;
No bird e'er breaks thy surface with his wing ;
No star, or sky, or bow, is ever glassed
Within thy depths ; no flower or blade e'er breathes
Its fragrance from thy bleak banks on the air.
True, here are flowers, or semblances of flowers,
Carved by the magic fingers of the drops
That fall upon thy rocky battlements—
Fair roses, tulips, pinks, and violets—
All white as cerements of the coffined dead ;
But they are flowers of stone, and never drank
The sunshine or the dew.   O somber stream,
Whence comest thou, and whither goest?   Far
Above, upon the surface of old Earth,
A hundred rivers o'er thee pass and sweep,
In music and in sunshine, to the sea ;—
Thou art not born of them.   Whence comest thou,

And whither goest? None of earth can know.
No mortal e'er has gazed upon thy source—
No mortal seen where thy dark waters blend
With the abyss of Ocean. None may guess
The mysteries of thy course. Perchance thou hast
A hundred mighty cataracts, thundering down
Toward Earth's eternal center; but their sound
Is not for ear of man. All we can know
Is that thy tide rolls out, a specter stream,
From yon stupendous, frowning wall of rock,
And, moving on a little way, sinks down
Beneath another mass of rock as dark
And frowning, even as life—our little life—
Born of one fathomless eternity,
Steals on a moment and then disappears
In an eternity as fathomless.

TO AN ABSENT WIFE.

'TIS Morn :—the sea-breeze seems to bring
    Joy, health, and freshness on its wing ;
Bright flowers, to me all strange and new,
Are glittering in the early dew,
And perfumes rise from every grove,
As incense to the clouds that move
Like spirits o'er yon welkin clear :
But I am sad—thou art not here !

'T is Noon :—a calm, unbroken sleep
Is on the blue waves of the deep
A soft haze, like a fairy dream,
Is floating over wood and stream ,
And many a broad magnolia flower,
Within its shadowy woodland bower,
Is gleaming like a lovely star :
But I am sad—thou art afar !

'T is Eve :—on earth the sunset skies
Are painting their own Eden dyes ;
The stars come down, and trembling glow
Like blossoms on the waves below ;

And, like an unseen spirit, the breeze
Seems lingering 'midst these orange trees,
Breathing its music round the spot:
But I am sad—I see thee not!

'T is Midnight :—with a soothing spell,
The far tones of the ocean swell,
Soft as a mother's cadence mild,
Low bending o'er her sleeping child;
And on each wandering breeze are heard
The rich notes of the mocking-bird,
In many a wild and wondrous lay:
But I am sad—thou art away!

I sink in dreams :—low, sweet, and clear,
Thy own dear voice is in my ear;
Around my neck thy tresses twine—
Thy own loved hand is clasped in mine—
Thy own soft lip to mine is pressed—
Thy head is pillowed on my breast :—
Oh! I have all my heart holds dear,
And I am happy—thou art here!

HARVEST HYMN.

At Carmel's mount the prophet laid
   His offering on the altar-stone,
And fire descended from the skies,
   And round the holy altar shone;
And thus, when Spring went smiling past,
Our offerings on the earth were cast,
And God's own blessing has come down,
Our sacrifice of faith to crown.

No conqueror o'er our fields has gone,
   To blast with war our summer bowers,
And stain with blood of woe and guilt,
   The soil that giveth life to flowers;
But morning dews and evening rains
Have fallen on our beauteous plains,
And earth, through all her realms abroad,
Gives back the image of her God.

Bright with the Autumn's richest tints,
   Each hill lifts up its head on high,
And spreads its fruits and blossoms out,
   An offering meet beneath the sky;

And hill, and plain, and vale, and grove,
Join in the sacrifice of love,
And wind, and stream, and lake, and sea,
Lift high their hymns of ecstasy.

It is the festival of earth—
  The flame of love o'er Nature burns,
And to the holy heavens goes up
  Like incense from a thousand urns;
And oh, let man's impassioned voice,
With Nature's self, in song rejoice,
Until the blended notes of love
Ring from the temple-arch above.

AN INFANT'S GRAVE.*

NOT in the church-yard's hallowed ground,
    Where marble columns rise around,
By willow or by cypress shade,
Are thy poor little relics laid.
Thou sleepest here, all, all alone—
No other grave is near thine own.
'T is well, 't is well ; but oh, such fate
Seems very, very desolate.

We know not whence thy little form
Was borne through rain, and wind, and storm ;
We know not to what far-off wild
They sought to take thee, lonely child.
We only know thy puny life
Was all unequal to the strife,
And that thy dust is sleeping here,
Unwet but by the stranger's tear.

*A few months ago, I stood in the forest of Arkansas, at the grave of an infant, buried from an emigrant's wagon.

Alas, what bitter tear-drops stole
From thy poor mother's stricken soul,
When in this dark and gloomy dell
The damp clods on thy bosom fell:
How throbbed her brain, how throbbed her heart,
When mournfully she turned to part
From the rude mound her dear one o'er,
To gaze upon it never more!

But yet it matters not, poor child,
That thou must sleep in this lone wild;
Each Spring-time, as it wanders past,
Its buds and blooms will round thee cast;
The thick-leaved boughs and moonbeams pale
Will o'er thee spread a solemn vail,
And softest dews and showers will lave
The blossoms on the infant's grave.

Farewell! I've paused one little hour
To plant, lone child, this humble flower
Above thy dust, and now I grieve
To leave thee as all others leave.
Farewell! farewell! where'er I stray,
This mournful scene will with me stay—
A picture hung upon the walls
Of memory's dim and somber halls.

THE ISLE AND STAR.

IN the tropical seas
   There's a beautiful isle,
Where storms never darken
   The sunlight's soft smile.
There the hymn of the breeze
   And the hymn of the stream
Are mingled in one,
   Like sweet sounds in a dream.
There the song-birds at morn
   From the thick shadows start,
Like musical thoughts
   From the poet's full heart.
There the song-birds at noon,
   Sit in silence unbroken,
Like an exquisite dream
   In the bosom, unspoken.
There the flowers hang like rainbows
   On wildwood and lea :—
O, say wilt thou dwell
   In that sweet isle with me?

In the depth of the sky
　There's a beautiful star,
Where no yew casts a shadow
　The bright scene to mar.
There the rainbows ne'er fade,
　And the dews are ne'er dry,
And a circle of moons
　Ever shines in the sky.
There the songs of the blest,
　And the songs of the spheres,
Are unceasingly heard
　Through the infinite years.
There the soft airs float down
　From the amaranth bowers,
All faint with the perfume
　Of Eden's own flowers.
There truth, love, and beauty
　Immortal will be :—
O, say, wilt thou dwell
　In that sweet star with me?

THE BOUQUET'S COMPLIMENTS.

TO thee, the pure, the bright, the good,
We come, a gentle sisterhood,
From many a sweet and lovely spot,
From wood and dell and fairy grot,
With dews from nature's diamond mine,
To worship at thy beauty's shrine,
And hail thee in this simple lay,
Our own enchanting Queen of May.

In our far homes by wood and dell
We often heard thy lovers tell
With gesture wild and frenzied start,
How very beautiful thou art.
They called thee sweeter, brighter far,
Than sweetest flower or brightest star ;
They said that language could not speak
The beauty of thy lip and cheek ;
They said the music of thy words
Was richer than the voice of birds ;
And we have come without a sigh
To see thee, hear thee, and to die.

And it is true, dear Queen of May,
All that we heard thy lovers say:
Our red rose, when with dews it drips,
Is not so red as thy red lips;
Our violet's bluer than the sky,
But not so blue as thy blue eye;
Our jasmine's breath, though deemed divine,
Is not so sweet, fair one, as thine;
The loveliest stars we used to see
Are dim and cold compared to thee;
And there 's no bird, in field or grove,
Can match thy gentle tones of love.

And now, dear Queen, accept, we pray,
The homage we have come to pay;
Our life, we know, is very brief,
But yet in joy, and not in grief,
Our lids will close if we may glow
Awhile upon thy bosom's snow,
Or die, O loveliest of girls,
In the warm sunshine of thy curls.

THE DEAD MARINER.

SLEEP on, sleep on ! above thy corse
 The winds their Sabbath keep ;
The waves are round thee, and thy breast
 Heaves with the heaving deep.
O'er thee, mild eve her beauty flings,
And there the white gull lifts her wings ;
And the blue halcyon loves to lave
Her plumage in the deep, blue wave.

Sleep on ! no willow o'er thee bends
 With melancholy air,
No violet springs, nor dewy rose
 Its soul of love lays bare ;
But there the sea-flower, bright and young,
Is sweetly o'er thy slumbers flung ;
And, like a weeping mourner fair,
The pale flag hangs its tresses there.

Sleep on, sleep on ! the glittering depths
 Of ocean's coral caves
Are thy bright urn—thy requiem
 The music of its waves ;

The purple gems forever burn
In fadeless beauty round thy urn ;
And, pure and deep as infant love,
The blue sea rolls its waves above.

Sleep on, sleep on ! the fearful wrath
 Of mingling cloud and deep
May leave its wild and stormy track
 Above thy place of sleep ;
But, when the wave has sunk to rest,
As now, 't will murmur o'er thy breast,
And the bright victims of the sea
Perchance will make their home with thee.

Sleep on ! thy corse is far away,
 But love bewails thee yet ;
For thee the heart-wrung sigh is breathed,
 And lovely eyes are wet ;
And she, thy young and beauteous bride,
Her thoughts are hovering by thy side,
As oft she turns to view, with tears,
The Eden of departed years.

THE STARS.

THOSE burning stars! what are they? I have dreamed
　　That they were blossoms from the tree of life,
Or glory flung back from the outspread wings
Of God's Archangels; or that yon blue skies,
With all their gorgeous blazonry of gems,
Were a bright banner waving o'er the earth
From the far wall of Heaven!　And I have sat
And drank their gushing glory, till I felt
Their flash electric trembling with the deep
And strong vibration down the living wire
Of chainless passion; and my every pulse
Was beating high, as if a spring were there
To buoy me up, where I might ever roam
'Mid the unfathomed vastness of the sky,
And dwell with those bright stars, and see their light
Poured down upon the sleeping earth like dew
From the bright urns of Naiads!
　　　　　　　　　　Beautiful stars!
What are ye?　There is in my heart of hearts
A fount that heaves beneath you, like the deep
Beneath the glories of the midnight moon!
And list!—your Eden-tones are floating now

Around me like an element : so slow,
So mildly beautiful, I almost deem
That ye are there, the living harps of God,
O'er which the incense-winds of Eden stray,
And wake such tones of mystic minstrelsy
As well might wander down to this dim world
To fashion dreams of Heaven ! Peal on, peal on,
Nature's high anthem ! for my life has caught
A portion of your purity and power,
And seems but as a sweet and glorious tone
Of wild star-music !

                 Blessed, blessed things !
Ye are in heaven, and I on earth. My soul,
Even with a whirlwind's rush, can wander off
To your immortal realms, but it must fall,
Like your own ancient Pleiad, from its height,
To dim its new-caught glories in the dust !
This earth is very beautiful. I love
Its wilderness of flowers, its bright clouds,
The majesty of mountains, and the dread
Magnificence of ocean—for they come
Like visions on my heart ; but when I look
On your unfading loveliness, I feel
Like a lost infant gazing on its home,
And weep to die, and come where ye repose
Upon your boundless heaven, like parted souls
On an eternity of blessedness.

OUR CHILDHOOD.

'TIS sad, yet sweet, to listen to the south wind's
    gentle swell,
And think we hear the music our childhood knew so
    well ;
To gaze out on the even, and the boundless fields of
    air,
And feel again our boyhood's wish to roam like angels
    there.

There are many dreams of gladness that cling around
    the Past,
And from the tomb of feeling old thoughts come throng-
    ing fast ;
The forms we loved so dearly in the happy days now
    gone,
The beautiful and lovely, so fair to look upon :—

Those bright and gentle maidens, who seemed so formed
    for bliss,
Too glorious and too heavenly for such a world as
    this—

Whose dark, soft eyes seemed swimming in a sea of
    liquid light,
And whose locks of gold were streaming o'er brows so
    sunny bright;

Whose smiles were like the sunshine in the spring-time
    of the year—
Like the changeful gleams of April, they followed every
    tear:
They have passed—like hopes—away, and their love-
    liness has fled;
Oh! many a heart is mourning that they are with the
    dead.
Like the brightest buds of summer, they have fallen
    with the stem;
Yet, oh, it is a lovely death, to fade from earth like
    them!

And yet the thought is saddening to muse on such as
    they,
And feel that all the beautiful are passing fast
    away;
That the fair ones whom we love grow to each loving
    breast
Like the tendril of the clinging vine, then perish
    where they rest.

And we can but think of these, in the soft and gentle
 Spring,
When the trees are waving o'er us, and the flowers are
 blossoming;
And we know that Winter's coming with his cold and
 stormy sky,
And the glorious beauty round us is budding but to
 die!

TO A YOUNG BEAUTY.

THAT dark, bright eye—that dark, bright eye—
   Where thoughts are pictured pure and high,
And love's young visions softly gleam
Like rose-tints on the twilight stream:
That dark, bright eye—oh, I have felt
   The witchery of its magic rare
Come o'er me till I could have knelt
   To worship the bright Spirit there.

That raven hair—that raven hair—
That wooes the soft and amorous air,
And o'er thy brow's pure whiteness flows
Like clouds o'er morning's drifted snows:
That raven hair—I love to mark
   Its clusters o'er thy temples rove,
While sweetly from its ringlets dark
   Is breathing all the soul of love.

That lovely cheek—that lovely cheek—
Where joy and beauty seem to speak
From every lineament, and twine
Their flower-wreaths o'er its virgin shrine:

That lovely cheek—how sweet to muse
　　On the dear tints that o'er it rise,
And, gazing on those breathing hues,
　　To dream of love and Paradise.

That floating form—that floating form—
With Heaven's own glowing spirit warm,
So beautiful, the vision fair
Seems a bright creature of the air:
That floating form—oh, I have dreamed
　　Such forms were in the bowers above—
Too bright for earth the vision seemed,
　　A thing of ecstasy and love.

A NAME IN THE SAND.

ALONE I walked the ocean strand;
 A pearly shell was in my hand:
I stooped and wrote upon the sand
 My name, the year and day :—
As onward from the spot I passed,
One lingering look behind I cast,—
A wave came rolling high and fast,
 And washed my line away.

And so, methought, 't will quickly be
With every mark on earth from me :
A wave of dark oblivion's sea,
 Will sweep across the place
Where I have trod the sandy shore
Of time, and been to be no more—
Of me, my day, the name I bore,
 To leave no track or trace.

And yet, with Him who counts the sands,
And holds the water in his hands,

I know a lasting record stands,
  Inscribed against my name,
Of all this mortal part has wrought,
Of all this thinking soul has thought,
And from these fleeting moments caught,
  For glory or for shame.

A DIRGE.

'TWAS her fourth birth-day, and the morning rose
    Bright as a dream of Eden, but she lay
Within her snow-white shroud in cold repose,
    A form of beautiful, unbreathing clay;
Sweet spring-flowers lay beside her in their bloom,
    And one unopened bud was in her hand,
An emblem of her doom—no, not *her* doom,
    For she will blossom in the better land.

She came, and passed to her bright home above
    Ere yet one cloud had darkened life's young springs,
Ere hope had faded in her heart, or love
    Within her soul had shut its wounded wings;
She was all truth, and love, and loveliness,
    And it is well such pure, sweet ones should die,—
Upon the earth there is a blossom less,
    But oh, there is an added star on high.

Though we be doomed a while on earth to stay,
    'T is sin to mourn when sinless beings die;

To grieve when earth's frail beauty fades away
    In the immortal beauty of the sky;
To murmur when the young and lovely wake
    From this dark sleep and all its tearful dreams,
And go, 'mid songs of cherub bands to take
    Their angel plumage by the Eden streams.

SENT WITH A ROSE.

OH, take my rose,—'t is a lovely flower,
   And 't was plucked in the morning's earliest hour,
When a dew-drop lay at its heart of pearl
Like a dream in the breast of a sleeping girl.

Oh, press my rose, at thy own sweet home,
Between the leaves of thy favorite tome;
Then keep it ever, for it will be
A token of love from my heart to thee.

There's a rose, dear lady, upon thy cheek,
Oh, fairer and brighter than words can speak;
But treasure this precept within thy breast,
By none, save me, must *that* rose be pressed.

SABBATH EVENING.

HOW calmly sinks the parting sun!
    Yet twilight lingers still;
And beautiful as dreams of Heaven
    It slumbers on the hill;
Earth sleeps, with all her glorious things,
Beneath the Holy Spirit's wings,
And, rendering back the hues above,
Seems resting in a trance of love.

Round yonder rocks, the forest trees
    *In shadowy groups recline,
Like saints at evening bowed in prayer
    Around their holy shrine;
And through their leaves the night-winds blow,
So calm and still, their music low
Seems the mysterious voice of prayer,
Soft echoed on the evening air.

And yonder western throng of clouds,
    Retiring from the sky,
So calmly move, so softly glow,
    They seem to Fancy's eye

Bright creatures of a better sphere,
Come down at noon to worship here,
And from their sacrifice of love
Returning to their home above.

The blue isles of the golden sea,
  The night-arch floating high,
The flowers that gaze upon the heavens,
  The bright streams leaping by,
Are living with religion ;—deep
On earth and sea its glories sleep,
And mingle with the starlight rays,
Like the soft light of parted days.

The spirit of the holy eve
  Comes through the silent air
To feeling's hidden spring, and wakes
  A gush of music there !
And the far depths of ether beam
So passing fair, we almost dream
That we can rise, and wander through
Their open paths of trackless blue.

Each soul is filled with glorious dreams,
  Each pulse is beating wild ;
And thought is soaring to the shrine
  Of glory undefiled !

And holy aspirations start,
Like blessed angels, from the heart,
And bind—for earth's dark ties are riven—
Our spirits to the gates of Heaven.

TO A LADY.

I THINK of thee when Morning springs
 From sleep with plumage bathed in dew,
And, like a young bird, lifts her wings
 Of gladness on the welkin blue.

And when, at noon, the breath of love
 O'er flower and stream is wandering free,
And sent in music from the grove,
 I think of thee, I think of thee.

I think of thee, when, soft and wide,
 The Evening spreads her robes of light,
And, like a young and timid bride,
 Sits blushing in the arms of Night.

And when the moon's sweet crescent springs
 In light o'er heaven's deep, waveless sea,
And stars are forth, like blessed things,
 I think of thee, I think of thee.

I think of thee :—that eye of flame,
    Those tresses, falling bright and free,
That brow, where " Beauty writes her name "—
    I think of thee, I think of thee.

ON REVISITING BROWN UNIVERSITY.

IT is the noon of night. On this calm spot,
  Where passed my boyhood's years, I sit me down
To wander through the dim world of the Past.

The Past! the silent Past! pale Memory kneels
Beside her shadowy urn, and with a deep
And voiceless sorrow weeps above the grave
Of beautiful affections. Her lone harp
Lies broken at her feet, and, as the wind
Goes o'er its moldering chords, a dirge-like sound
Rises upon the air, and all again
Is an unbreathing silence.
                            Oh, the Past!
Its spirit as a mournful presence lives
In every ray that gilds those ancient spires,
And like a low and melancholy wind
Comes o'er yon distant wood, and faintly breathes
Upon my fevered spirit. Here I roved
Ere I had fancied aught of life beyond
The poet's twilight imaging. Those years
Come o'er me like the breath of fading flowers,
And tones I loved fall on my heart as dew

Upon the withered rose-leaf.   They were years
When the rich sunlight blossomed in the air,
And fancy, like a blessed rainbow, spanned
The waves of Time, and joyous thoughts went off
Upon its beautiful unpillared arch
To revel there in cloud, and sun, and sky.

Within yon silent domes, how many hearts
Are beating high with glorious dreams. 'T is well;
The rosy sunlight of the morn should not
Be darkened by the portents of the storm
That may not burst till eve.   Those youthful ones,
Whose thoughts are woven of the hues of heaven,
May see their visions fading tint by tint,
Till naught is left upon the darkened air
Save the gray winter cloud; the brilliant star
That glitters now upon their happy lives
May redden to a scorching flame and burn
Their every hope to dust; yet why should thoughts
Of coming sorrows cloud their hearts' bright depths
With an untimely shade?   Dream on—dream on,
Ye thoughtless ones—dream on while yet ye may !
When life is but a shadow, tear, and sigh,
Ye will turn back to linger round these hours
Like stricken pilgrims, and their music sweet
Will be a dear though melancholy tone
In Memory's ear, sounding forever more.

CLOSE OF THE YEAR 1832.

L IKE a swift wave, the dying year
   Down Time's dark flood has passed,
And its last sigh is lingering now
   Upon the sinking blast;
Oh, while it sparkled in the sun,
It mirrored glories one by one,
   Too beautiful to last;
And these, lone year, are fled, like thee,
To the dim past's unfathom'd sea

How many a change is ours !—the young,
   Like Spring's fresh flowers, have died,
And manhood, like the Summer's flash,
   Has faded in his pride;
And aged ones, like withered leaves,
Through which the Autumn tempest grieves,
   Have fallen, side by side;
The wild wind wails o'er earth to-day
The dirge of millions passed away.

These stanzas were written (but not published) on the 31st of December, 1832. In that year Sir Walter Scott and Charles Carroll of Carrollton died, and South Carolina Nullification threatened the dissolution of the American Union.

CLOSE OF THE YEAR 1832.

Even he, the monarch of the heart,
   The gifted and the proud,
The wizard of old Scotland's hills,
   In common dust is bowed—
He, who on Mind's high steep could stand,
And marshal with his sceptered hand
   The whirlwind and the cloud,
And write a name, too bright to die,
In lightning-traces on the sky.

In our own land has fallen one,
   Whose fame at Time will mock—
Who set his name to Freedom's scroll,
   And dared the battle-shock ;
The last of that proud band lies low
That bared their bosoms to the foe,
   A living rampart rock,
And stood, the prophets of the free,
At Liberty's Thermopylæ.

Gone is our Spartan phalanx now—
   In vain were tear and prayer—
But list ! their awful voices still
   Breathe, burn upon the air !
They ring upon their country's ear
A tone of warning and of fear,
   And bid her sons beware,
Nor madly quench the glorious star,
That nations worship from afar.

Time rushes still: another year,
   Like that whose tale is told,
Is hurrying wildly past—and what
   Will its dark months unfold!
Like bale-fires on a stormy sea,
Visions of blood perchance will be
   Upon its chart unrolled;
And strife may whet the sword of doom
E'en on the stone of Carroll's tomb.

A signal in the midnight heavens!
   Lo, where yon meteor-gleam
Is flashing from the far-off South
   To old Potomac's stream!
Its lurid and portentous smile
Is like that star o'er Patmos' isle,
   Seen in the Prophet's dream,
That sank on hill, and vale, and flood,
And turned earth's waters into blood.

My country, oh my country, pause
   Ere guilt has stained thy hand,
Pause 'mid thy perils, and invoke
   The God of Freedom's land;
Then if the war-cloud vail thy sun.
The spirit of thy Washington
   Upon that cloud will stand,
To scatter its red folds in air
And bend the bow of glory there.

ANNIVERSARY OF A FRIEND'S WEDDING.

WE'VE shared each other's smiles and tears
 Through years of wedded life;
And Love has blessed those fleeting years,
 My own, my cherished wife.

And if, at times, the storm's dark shroud
 Has rested in the air,
Love's beaming sun has kissed the cloud,
 And left the rainbow there.

In all our hopes, in all our dreams,
 Love is forever nigh,—
A blossom in our path it seems,
 A sunbeam in our sky.

"One morning while suffering in this way [from paralysis of his writing fingers], he composed a beautiful song for his friend, Dr. T. S. Bell. Mr. Prentice's amanuensis was not in, and he stepped over to the Doctor's office, and asked him to write something for him, saying: "It is for you and your wife." Mr. Prentice then dictated the following beautiful lines, which were afterward set to music by a distinguished artist of Poland."— *G. W. Griffin.*

For all our joys of brightest hue
   Grow brighter in Love's smile,
And there's no grief our hearts e'er knew
   That Love could not beguile.

MEMORIES.

ONCE more, once more, my Mary dear,
   I sit by that lone stream,
Where first within thy timid ear
   I breathed love's burning dream.
The birds we loved still tell their tale
   Of music, on each spray,
And still the wild-rose decks the vale —
   But thou art far away.

In vain thy vanished form I seek,
   By wood and stream and dell,
And tears of anguish bathe my cheek
   Where tears of rapture fell;
And yet beneath those wild-wood bowers
   Dear thoughts my soul employ,
For in the memories of past hours
   There is a mournful joy.

Upon the air thy gentle words
   Around me seem to thrill,
Like sounds upon the wind harp's chords
   When all the winds are still,

Or like the low and soul-like swell
   Of that wild spirit-tone,
Which haunts the hollow of the bell
   When its sad chime is done.

I seem to hear thee speak my name
   In sweet, low murmurs now ;
I seem to feel thy breath of flame
   Upon my cheek and brow ;
On my cold lips I feel thy kiss,
   Thy heart to mine is laid—
Alas, that such a dream of bliss
   Like other dreams must fade !

MAMMOTH CAVE.

ALL day, as day is reckoned on the earth,
 I've wandered in these dim and awful aisles,
Shut from the blue and breezy dome of heaven,
While thoughts, wild, drear, and shadowy, have swept
Across my awe-struck soul, like specters o'er
The wizard's magic glass, or thunder-clouds
O'er the blue waters of the deep. And now
I'll sit me down upon yon broken rock
To muse upon the strange and solemn things
Of this mysterious realm.
       All day my steps
Have been amid the beautiful, the wild,
The gloomy, the terrific. Crystal founts,
Almost invisible in their serene
And pure transparency ; high, pillared domes,
With stars and flowers all fretted like the halls
Of Oriental monarchs ; rivers dark
And drear and voiceless as Oblivion's stream,
That flows through Death's dim vale of silence ; gulfs
All fathomless, down which the loosened rock
Plunges until its far-off echoes come

Fainter and fainter like the dying roll
Of thunders in the distance; Stygian pools
Whose agitated waves give back a sound
Hollow and dismal, like the sullen roar
In the volcano's depths :—these, these have left
Their spell upon me, and their memories
Have passed into my spirit, and are now
Blent with my being till they seem a part
Of my own immortality.

             God's hand,
At the creation, hollowed out this vast
Domain of darkness, where no herb nor flower
E'er sprang amid the sands, nor dews, nor rains,
Nor blessed sunbeams fell with freshening power,
Nor gentle breeze its Eden message told
Amid the dreadful gloom. Six thousand years
Swept o'er the earth ere human footprints marked
This subterranean desert. Centuries
Like shadows came and past, and not a sound
Was in this realm, save when at intervals,
In the long lapse of ages, some huge mass
Of overhanging rock fell thundering down,
Its echoes sounding through these corridors
A moment, and then dying in a hush
Of silence, such as brooded o'er the earth
When earth was chaos. The great mastodon,
The dreaded monster of the elder world,

Passed o'er this mighty cavern, and his tread
Bent the old forest oaks like fragile reeds
And made earth tremble ; armies in their pride
Perchance have met above it in the shock
Of war, with shout and groan, and clarion blast,
And the hoarse echoes of the thunder gun ;
The storm, the whirlwind, and the hurricane
Have roared above it, and the bursting cloud
Sent down its red and crashing thunderbolt ;
Earthquakes have trampled o'er it in their wrath,
Rocking earth's surface as the storm-wind rocks
The old Atlantic ;—yet no sound of these
E'er came down to the everlasting depths
Of these dark solitudes.
                         How oft we gaze
With awe or admiration on the new
And unfamiliar, but pass coldly by
The lovelier and the mightier ! Wonderful
Is this lone world of darkness and of gloom,
But far more wonderful yon outer world
Lit by the glorious sun.   These arches swell
Sublime in lone and dim magnificence,
But how sublimer God's blue canopy,
Beleaguered with his burning cherubim
Keeping their watch eternal ! Beautiful
Are all the thousand snow-white gems that lie
In these mysterious chambers, gleaming out

Amid the melancholy gloom, and wild
These rocky hills and cliffs and gulfs, but far
More beautiful and wild the things that greet
The wanderer in our world of light: the stars
Floating on high like islands of the blest;
The autumn sunsets glowing like the gate
Of far-off Paradise; the gorgeous clouds
On which the glories of the earth and sky
Meet and commingle; earth's unnumbered flowers
All turning up their gentle eyes to heaven;
The birds, with bright wings glancing in the sun,
Filling the air with rainbow miniatures;
The green old forests surging in the gale;
The everlasting mountains, on whose peaks
The setting sun burns like an altar-flame;
And ocean, like a pure heart rendering back
Heaven's perfect image, or in his wild wrath
Heaving and tossing like the stormy breast
Of a chained giant in his agony.

TO SUE.

'TIS very sweet to sit and gaze, dear girl,
　　On thy fair face,
As glowing as a crimson-shaded pearl
　　Or lighted vase.
Young beauty brightens, like an Eden-dream,
　　On thy pure cheek,
And joy and love from every feature seem
　　To breathe and speak.

I love to kneel in worship to the Sprite
　　In thy dark eyes,
Dark as the fabled Stygian stream, and bright
　　As Paradise.
Not oft the radiance of such eyes is given
　　To light our way;
And oh, to me there's not a star in heaven
　　So bright as they.

I've known thee but a few brief days, and yet
　　Thou wilt remain
An image of undying beauty set
　　On heart and brain.

Each thought, each dream of thee, fair girl, will seem
 Mid toil and strife,
A pure white lily swaying on the stream
 Of this dark life.

The months will pass, the flowers will soon be bright
 On plain and hill,
And the young birds with voices of delight.
 The woodlands fill ;
Oh, in that fairy season thou shalt be—
 Mid budding bowers—
My heart's young May-queen, and I 'll twine for thee
 The heart's wild flowers.

May fortune's richest gifts be hourly strewn
 Around thy feet ;
May every sound that greets thee be a tone
 Of music sweet.
May every blessing rest upon thy heart
 Like morning dew,
And no sad tear e'er from thy eyelids start,
 My gentle Sue.

ON A WARM DAY NEAR THE CLOSE OF WINTER.

HOW soft this southern gale ! Its freshness falls
   Upon my forehead like the light, warm touch
Of the dew-lips of Spring-time. It has been
In the far clime of blossoms, and it bears
A message of affection to our woods,
And vales, and streams. Spring, with her rose-air breath,
Is coming now upon her rainbow wing,
To waken the green earth to life and joy,
And the free air to music. She will weave
Her violet throne upon a thin, white cloud,
Soft floating in the middle-air, and call
Upon her thousand votaries to hail
Her coming with a song and smile. The waves
Will shout from rock and mountain, the blue lakes
Will tremble like the plumage of a dove
In the new gush of sun-light, and the birds
Will breathe their loves in music, and float off—
A shower of blossoms in the atmosphere.
The young, gay leaves will weave their twilight hues
In grove and forest ; 'mid yon budding isles

The sea will sleep like a Circassian bride
Decked with her richest jewelry ; the sky
Will take a bluer tint, and seem to arch
More high and pure and beautiful above,
As if to let the spirit go abroad
In ampler journeyings ; and a deep spell
Of life and bliss will, like a blessing, rest
Upon the waking heart, and bid it float
Like a young flower upon the buoyant wave
Of beautiful imaginings of Heaven.

A WISH.

IN Southern seas, there is an isle,
　Where earth and sky forever smile ;
Where storms cast not their somber hue
Upon the welkin's holy blue ;
Where clouds of blessed incense rise
From myriad flowers of myriad dyes,
And strange, bright birds glance through the bowers,
Like wingéd stars or wingéd flowers.

Oh, dear one, would it were our lot
To dwell upon that lovely spot ;
To stray through woods with blossoms starred,
Bright as the dreams of seer or bard ;
To hear each other's whispered words
'Mid the wild notes of tropic birds,
And deem our lives, in those bright bowers,
One glorious dream of love and flowers.

TO THE DAUGHTER OF AN OLD SWEETHEART.

I LOVE thee, Juliet, for thy mother's sake,
 And were I young should love thee for thine own.
Afresh in thee her early charms awake,
 And all her witcheries are round thee thrown ;
Thine are her girlhood's features, and I know
Her many virtues in thy bosom glow.

Thou art as lovely, though not yet as famed,
 As that bright maid, the beautiful, the true,
The gentle being for whom thou wast named,
 The Juliet that our glorious Shakspeare drew.
Thine is her magic loveliness—but, oh,
What fiery youth shall be thy Romeo?

Whoe'er he be, oh, may his lot and thine
 Be happier than the lot of those of old ;
May ye, like them, bow low at passion's shrine,
 May love within your bosoms ne'er grow cold ;
And may your paths be ne'er, like theirs, beset
By strifes of Montague and Capulet.

Like his great prototype, thy Romeo,
 Half-frenzied by his passion's raging flame,
And kindling with a poet's fervid glow,
 May fancy he might cut thy beauteous frame
Into bright stars to deck the midnight sky—
But, gentle Juliet, may he never try!

I paid the tribute of an humble lay
 To thy fair mother in her girlhood bright,
And now this humbler offering I pay
 To thee, oh, sweet young spirit of delight.
And may I not, tossed on life's stormy waters,
Live to make rhymes, dear Juliet, to thy daughters?

THE GRAVE OF THE BEAUTIFUL.

'TIS twilight, and I stand beside her grave !
   Her grave ! Alas, that so much loveliness
Should sink into the damp, cold earth ! Alas,
That beauty such as hers should pass away,
And that its image should exist no more
Save in the hearts of mourning ones !

                         Oh, she
Was beautiful as some bright, wingéd dream
That wanders down from Eden's blessed bowers,
And folds its starry plumes within the soul
Of musing bard or sculptor. Forms like hers
Oft pass at eve before the half-closed-eye—
They glide like shadows o'er our paths, or bend
From the soft edges of a moonlight cloud,
And beckon to the sky, but rarely come
Like her to beautify our homes and hearths
With their abiding smiles.

                  I see her now,
Her blue eye floating in its own clear light,

Her young cheek, bright as an illumined gem,
Her red lips, parted in their mirth, her smile
Beaming like sunshine from each lineament,
Her light step bounding o'er the summer flowers
In very joyousness, as if she were
A spirit of the morning or a wild
Glad creature of the air—and can it be
That all that bright exuberance of life,
And love, and happiness, is sleeping now
In deep and dark decay? Oh, can it be
That Spring, with her soft skies, will come again,
And by her warm breath woo her violets
And roses from the earth, and send her streams
Leaping and singing to the sea, and fill
The soft air with her thousand melodies
Of bird and breeze, and grove and waterfall,
And our loved lost one be not here to greet
With us the glories of the vernal time,
And blend her ringing cadences with all
The harmonies of Nature in her joy?

MY HEART IS WITH THEE.

WHEN the breeze with a whisper
  Steals soft through the grove,
A sweet earnest lisper
 Of music and love ;
When its gentle caressings
 Away charm each sigh,
And the still dews, like blessings,
 Descend from the sky ;
When a deep spell is lying
 On hill, vale, and lea—
My warm heart is flying,
 Sweet spirit, to thee.

When stars like sky-blossoms
 Above seem to blow,
And waves like young bosoms
 Are swelling below ;
When the voice of the river
 Floats mournfully past,

And the forest's low shiver
 Is borne on the blast ;
When wild tones are swelling
 From earth, air, and sea—
My warm heart is dwelling,
 Sweet spirit, with thee.

When the night-clouds are riding,
 Like ghosts, on the gale,
And the young moon is gliding,
 Sweet, lonely, and pale ;
When the ocean is sobbing
 In ceaseless unrest,
And its great heart is throbbing
 All wild in its breast ;
When the strong wind is wrestling
 With billow and tree—
My warm heart is nestling,
 Sweet spirit, with thee.

When in slumber thy fancies
 In loveliness gleam,
And a thousand romances
 Are bright in thy dream ;
When visions of brightness
 Like young angels start

In beautiful lightness
  All wild from thy heart;
When thy calm sleep is giving
  Thy dream-wings to thee,
Oh, say art thou living,
  Sweet spirit, with me?

MY MOTHER.

MY mother, 't is a long and weary time
Since last I looked upon thy sad, sweet face,
And listened to the gentle spirit-tones
Of thy dear voice of music. I was then
A child, a bright-haired child. The fearful thought
Which slowly fastened on my throbbing brain,
That thou wast passing from the earth away,
Was my young life's first sorrow. Through the long
And solemn watches of that awful night,
Kind friends, who dearly loved us, gathered round
Thy dying couch, and, in my agony,
I shrieked to them to save thee ; but with tears,
And in the tones of holy sympathy,
They told me thou wouldst die.
     Ah, then I bowed
My head to God, whose worship thy dear lips
Had taught me, and to Him with bursting heart
I prayed that He would spare thee. And, as there
I knelt, a holy calm, as if from Heaven,

Came stealing o'er my spirit, and a voice
Floated into my soul.   It said that thou
Must leave me, that thy home was in the sky,
But that thou still wouldst love and guard thy child,
And hover round him on thy angel-wings
In all his wanderings here.

     My mother, then
I rose in more than childhood's strength, and watched
The fading of thy life.   Dear friends still hung
Around thy pillow, but I saw them not.
Wild lamentations and deep sobs were breathed
From hearts of anguish, but I heard them not.
A man of God poured forth his soul in prayer
For thy soul's welfare, but I heard him not.
I saw but thy wan cheek, thy parted lips,
Thy half-closed eyes, so meek and calm beneath
Their blue-veined lids ; thy bright, disheveled locks,
Thy pallid brow, damp with the dews of death,
And the faint heaving of thy breast, that oft
In happy hours had pillowed my young head
To sweet and gentle slumber ; and I heard
But the faint struggle of thy failing breath,
Thy stifling sighs, and the high, holy words
That seemed to fall like dew-drops on my soul
From out the blessed skies.   All suddenly
Thy dark eyes opened, and a moment looked
Upon thy child with one fixed, burning gaze,

In which the deep and hoarded love of years
Was all concentred ; a convulsive thrill
Shot through the fibres of thy wasted frame ;
And Death was there—aye, thou wast mine and Death's ;
And then my tears again gushed wildly forth ;
But light from Heaven broke through them with a soft
Prismatic glory, as I gazed above,
And saw thee mounting, like a new-made star,
Far up thy glowing pathway in the heavens.

Long years, my dear, lost mother, have gone by
Since thy death-hour.   My childhood and my youth
Have passed since then, and my strong manhood's prime
Has faded like a vision, for my years
Far, far outnumber thine on earth.   I 've seen
Much, much of joy and sorrow ; I have felt
Life's storms and sunshine, but I ne'er have known
Such raptures as my full heart shared with thee
In childhood's fairy years.   Now, Time no more
Scatters fresh roses round my feet ;—his hand
Lets fall upon my path but pale, torn flowers,
Dead blossoms, that the gentle dews of eve,
The morning sunlight and the noontide rains
Can ne'er revive.   E'en thy dear image now,
The sunlight of my childhood, seems to fade
From Memory's vision.   'T is as some pale tint
Upon the twilight wave, a broken glimpse

Of something beautiful and dearly loved
In far-gone years; a dim and tender dream,
That, like a faint bow on a darkened sky,
Lies on my clouded brain. But, oh! thy voice—
Its tones can never perish in my soul;
It visits me amid the strife of men
In the dark city's solitude. It comes,
Amid the silence of the midnight hour,
Upon my listening spirit like a strain
Of fairy music o'er the sea. And oft,
When at the eventide, amid a hush
Deep as the awful stillness of a dream,
I stray all lonely through the leafless woods,
And gaze upon the moon that seems to mourn
Her lonely lot in heaven, or on the trees,
That look like frowning Titans in the dim
And doubtful light, that unforgotten voice
Swells on my ear like the low mournful tone
Imprisoned in the sea-shell, or the sound,
The melancholy sound, of dying gales
Panting upon the far-off tree-tops.
                                    Yes,
My mother dear, though mountains, hills and streams
Divide me from thy grave, where I so oft
In childhood laid my bosom on the turf
That covered thine; though the drear winter storms
Long, long have cast o'er thee their spotless shrouds,

And Night her pall, and though thine image sweet,
The one dear picture cherished through my life,
Grows dim and dimmer in my brain, thy voice
Is ever in my ear and in my heart,
To teach me love and gentleness and truth,
And warn me from the perils that surround
The paths of pilgrims o'er this desert earth.

MARY.

AGAIN the bright and joyous Spring
    Is passing o'er the earth,
And at her call the woodlands ring
    With melody and mirth.
Her music gushes from the stream
    And lingers in the bough,
And Nature seems a fairy dream—
    But, Mary, where art thou?

The flowers that faded from our sight
    In Autumn's chilling gale,
Again like earthly stars are bright
    On hill and plain and vale.
The violet thy dear fingers nursed
    Lifts up its timid brow,
And rose and lily bloom as erst—
    But, Mary, where art thou?

The many glories of the Spring,
    Its music and its flowers,
Back on my saddened spirit bring
    The thoughts of perished hours.

The joy that had its source in thee
  Seems stealing o'er me now:
Alas! 'tis all a mockery—
  Sweet Mary, where art thou?

Oh, bright ones still, though thou art fled,
  Around my pathway shine,
With eyes as blue and lips as red,
  And cheeks as fair as thine;
And still to these, 'mid mirth and song
  Proud men in worship bow:
Alas! I can not join the throng—
  Dear Mary, where art thou?

Oft-times in solitude afar,
  Where sin and strife are not,
I look on every lovely star
  To seek thy dwelling-spot;
Oh, many round the midnight throne
  Are burning brightly now,
But I would gaze on thine alone—
  Dear Mary, where art thou?

TO A BUNCH OF ROSES.

SWEET flowers, whilst ye impart
 The fragrance of the spring-time, rich and rare,
Go, bear that errand to young Julia's heart,
 Which only roses bear.

 Go, tell her, lovely flowers,
That in my soul her own dear image gleams,
A light, a radiance in my waking hours,
 A glory in my dreams.

 Say, though my love is hers,
To her alone I can that love reveal ;
Among her many burning worshipers
 I would, but may not kneel.

 Tell her it were your bliss
Upon her gentle bosom to repose,
And she, perhaps, may give you one sweet kiss—
 Oh, that I were a rose !

A NIGHT IN JUNE.

NIGHT steals upon the world; the shades,
  With silent flight, are sweeping down,
To steep, as day's last glory fades,
  In tints of blue the landscape brown;
The wave breaks not; deep slumber holds
The dewy leaves; the night-wind folds
Her melancholy wing; and sleep
Is forth upon the pulseless deep.

The willows, mid the silent rocks,
  Are brooding o'er the waters mild,
Like a fond mother's pendent locks
  Hung sweetly o'er her sleeping child;
The flowers that fringe the purple stream
Are sinking to their evening dream;
And earth appears a lovely spot,
Where Sorrow's voice awakens not.

But see! such pure, such beautiful,
  And burning scenes awake to birth
In yon bright depths, they render dull
  The loveliest tints that mantle earth!

The heavens are rolling blue and fair,
And the soft night-gems clustering there
Seem, as on high they breathe and burn,
Bright blossoms o'er day's shadowy urn.

At this still hour, when starry songs
    Are floating through night's glowing noon,
How sweet to view those radiant throngs
    Glitter around the throne of June!
To see them in their watch of love
Gaze from the holy heavens above,
And in their robes of brightness roam
Like angels o'er the eternal dome!

Their light is on the ocean isles,
    'T is trembling on the mountain stream;
And the far hills, beneath their smiles,
    Seem creatures of a blessed dream!
Upon the deep their glory lies,
As if untreasured from the skies,
And comes soft-flashing from its waves,
Like sea-gems from their sparry caves!

   *   *   *   *   *   *

Why gaze I thus?—'t is worse than vain!
    'T was here I gazed in years gone by,
Ere life's cold winds had breathed one stain
    On Fancy's rich and mellow sky.

I feel, I feel those early years
Deep thrilling through the fount of tears,
And hurrying brightly, wildly back
O'er Memory's deep and burning track !

'T was here I gazed ! The night-bird still
    Pours its sweet song ; the starlight beams
Still tinge the flower and forest hill ;
    And music gushes from the streams ;
But I am changed ! I feel no more
The sinless joys that charmed before ;
And the dear years, so far departed,
Come but to " mock the broken-hearted ! "

LINES TO A LADY.

LADY, I've gazed on thee,
And thou art now a vision of the Past,
A spirit-star, whose holy light is cast
On memory's voiceless sea.

That star—it lingers there
As beautiful as 't were a dewy flower,
Soft-wafted down from Eden's glorious bower,
And floating in mid-air.

It is, that blessed one,
The day-star of my destiny—the first
I e'er could worship as the Persian erst
Worshiped his own loved sun.

On all my years may lie
The shadow of the tempest, their dark flow
Be wild and drear, but that dear star will glow
Still beautiful on high.

BIRTH-DAY REFLECTIONS.

IT will be over soon.   Another year
   Is gone, and its low knell is tolling now
O'er the wide ocean of the Past.
                                        Alas!
I am not as in boyhood.   There were hours
Of joyousness that came like angel-shapes
Upon my heart, but they are altered now,
And rise on Memory's view like statues pale
By a dim fount of tears.   And there were streams
Upon whose breasts the sweet young blossoms leaned,
To list the gush of music, but their depths
Are turned to dust.   There, too, were blessed lights
That shone, sweet rainbows of the spirit, o'er
The skies of new existence, but their gleams,
Like the lost Pleiad of the olden time,
Have faded from the zenith, and are lost
'Mid earth's cold mockeries!
                                How all is changed!
The guardians of my young and sinless years
No more are dwellers of the earth.   Their tones

Of love oft dwell upon the twilight breeze,
Or wander sweetly down through mists and dews,
At midnight's calm and melancholy hour,
But voice alone is there ! Ages of thought
Come o'er me then, and, with a spirit won
Back to my earlier years, I kneel again
At young life's broken shrine.
     The thirst of power
Has been a fever to my spirit. Oft,
Even in my boyhood, I was wont to gaze
Upon the awful cataract rushing down
With its eternal thunder peal, the lone
Expanse of Ocean with its infinite
Of dark blue waters roaring to the heavens,
The night-storm fiercely rending the great oaks
From their rock-pinnacles, the giant-clouds
Waving their plumes like warriors in the sky,
And darting their quick lightning through the air
Like the red flash of swords—aye, I was wont
To gaze on these and almost weep to think
I could not match their strength. The same wild thirst
For power is yet upon me ; it has been
A madness in my day-dreams, and a curse
Upon my being ; it has led me on
To mingle in the strife of men ; and now
A myriad foes have left upon my name
The stain of their vile breaths.

Well, be it so!
There is a silent purpose in my heart,
And neither love, nor hate, nor fear shall quell
That one fixed daring. Though my being's stream
Gives forth no music now, 't is passing back
To its great fountain in the skies, and there
'T will rest forever in the ocean-tide
Of God's immensity. I will not mourn
Life's shrouded memories. I can still drink in
The unshadowed beauties of the universe,
Gaze with a soul of pride upon the blue
Magnificence above, and hear the hymns
Of Heaven in all the starry beams, and fill
Glen, vale, and wood and mountain with the bright
And glorious visions poured from the deep home
Of an immortal mind. Past year, farewell!

THE INVALID'S REPLY.

YES, dear one, I am dying.   Hope at times
    Has whispered to me, in her siren tones,
But now, alas ! I feel the tide of life
Fast ebbing from my heart.   I know that soon
The green and flowery curtain of the grave
Will close as softly round my fading form
As the calm shadows of the evening hour
Close o'er the fading stream.

                 Oh ! there are times
When my heart's tears gush wildly at the thought
That, in the fresh, young morning-tide of life,
I must resign my breath.   To me the earth
Is very beautiful.   I love its flowers,
Its birds, its dews, its rainbows, its glad streams,
Its vales, its mountains, its green, wooing woods,
Its moonlight clouds, its sunsets, and its soft
And dewy twilights ; and I needs must mourn
To think that I so soon shall pass away,
And see them nevermore.

                But thou, the loved
And fondly cherished idol of my life,

Thou dear twin-spirit of my deathless soul,
'T will be the keenest anguish of my heart
To part from thee.   True, we have never loved
With the wild passion that fills heart and brain
With flame and madness, yet my love for thee
Is my life's life.   A deeper, holier love
Has never sighed and wept beneath the stars,
Or glowed within the breasts of saints in heaven.
It does not seem a passion of my heart,
It is a portion of my soul.   I feel
That I am but a softened shade of thee,
And that my spirit, parted from thine own,   .
Might fade and perish from the universe
Like a star-shadow when the star itself
Is hidden by the storm-cloud.   Aye, I fear
That Heaven itself, though filled with love and God,
Will be to me all desolate, if thou,
Dear spirit, art not there.   I 've often prayed
That I might die before thee, for I felt
I could not dwell without thee on the earth,
And now my heart is breaking at the thought
Of dying while thou livest, for I feel,
My life's dear idol, that I can not dwell
Without thee in the sky.   Yet well I know
That love like ours, so holy, pure and high,
So far above the passions of the earth,
Can perish not with mortal life.   In Heaven

'T will brighten to a lovely star, and glow
In the far ages of eternity,
More beautiful and radiant than when first
'T was kindled into glory. Oh! I love,
I dearly love thee—these will be my last,
My dying words upon the earth, and they
Will be my first when we shall meet in Heaven;
And when ten thousand myriads of years
Shall fade into the past eternity,
My soul will breathe the same dear words to thine—
I love thee, oh! I love thee!
                  Weak and low
My pulse of life is fluttering at my heart,
And soon 't will cease forever. These faint words
Are the last echoes of the spirit's chords,
Stirred by the breath of Memory. Bear me, love,
I pray thee, to yon open window now,
That I may look once more on Nature's face
And listen to her gentle music-tone—
Her holy voice of love. How beautiful,
How very beautiful, are earth and sea,
And the o'erarching sky, to one whose eyes
Are soon to close upon the scenes of Time!
Yon blue lake sleeps beneath the flower-crowned hill
With his sweet picture on her breast; the white
And rosy clouds are floating through the air
Like cars of happy spirits; every leaf

And flower is colored by the crimson hues
Of the rich sunset, as the heart is tinged
By thoughts of Paradise ; and the far trees
Seem as if leaning, like departed souls,
Upon the holy heavens.   And look ! oh look !
Yon lovely star, the glorious evening star,
Is shining there, far, far above the mists
And dews of earth, like the bright star of faith
Above our mortal tears ! I ne'er before
Beheld the earth so green, the sky so blue,
The sunset and the star of eve so bright,
And soft, and beautiful ; I never felt
The dewy twilight breeze so calm and fresh
Upon my cheek and brow ; I never heard
The melodies of wind, and bird, and wave,
Fall with such sweetness on the ear.   I know
That Heaven is full of glory, but a God
Of love and mercy will forgive the tears,
Wrung from the fountain of my frail young heart,
By the sad thought of parting with the bright
And lovely things of earth.
               And, dear one, now
I feel that my poor heart must bid farewell
To thine.   Oh ! no, no, dearest ! not farewell,
For oft I will be with thee on the earth,
Although my home be Heaven.   At eventide
When thou art wandering by the silent stream,

To muse upon the sweet and mournful Past,
I will walk with thee, hand in hand, and share
Thy gentle thoughts and fancies; in thy grief,
When all seems dark and desolate around
Thy bleak and lonely pathway, I will glide
Like a bright shadow o'er thy soul, and charm
Away thy sorrow; in the quiet hush
Of the deep night, when thy dear head is laid
Upon thy pillow, and thy spirit craves
Communion with my spirit, I will come
To nerve thy heart with strength, and gently lay
My lip upon thy forehead with a touch
Like the soft kisses of the southern breeze
Stealing o'er bowers of roses; when the wild,
Dark storms of life beat fiercely on thy head,
Thou wilt behold my semblance on the cloud,
A rainbow to thy spirit; I will bend
At times above the fount within thy soul,
And thou wilt see my image in its depths,
Gazing into thy dark eyes with a smile
As I have gazed in life. And I will come
To thee in dreams, my spirit-mate, and we,
With clasping hands and interwining wings,
Will nightly wander o'er the starry deep,
And by the blessed streams of Paradise,
Loving in Heaven as we have loved on earth.

COME TO ME IN DREAMS.

COME in beautiful dreams, love,
  Oh! come to me oft,
When the light wings of sleep
  On my bosom lie soft;
Oh! come when the sea,
  In the moon's gentle light,
Beats low on the ear
  Like the pulse of the night;
When the sky and the wave
  Wear their holiest blue,
When the dew's on the flower
  And the star on the dew.

Come in beautiful dreams, love,
  Oh! come and we'll stray
Where the whole year is crowned
  With the blossoms of May;
Where each sound is as sweet
  As the coo of a dove,
And the gales are as soft
  As the breathing of love;

Where the beams kiss the waves,
  And the waves kiss the beach,
And our warm lips shall catch
  The sweet lessons they teach.

Come in beautiful dreams, love,
  Oh! come and we'll fly
Like two wingéd spirits
  Of love through the sky;
With hand clasped in hand
  On our dream-wings we'll go
Where the starlight and moonlight
  Are blending their glow;
And on bright clouds we'll linger
  Of purple and gold,
Till love's angels envy
  The bliss they behold.

TO ROSA.

NOT in the Grecian isles,
　　Not where the bright flowers of Illyssus shine,
E'er moved a breathing form whose beauty's wiles
　　Could match with thine.

Not where the golden glow
　　Of Italy's clear sky is pure and clear,
Not where the beauteous waves of Leman flow,
　　Hast thou thy peer.

Not where the sunlight falls
　　On bright Circassia through the perfumed air,
Nor in old Stamboul's oriental halls,
　　Dwells one so fair.

No fabled form of old,
　　Not hers who rose from out the foaming sea,
Though deemed more fair than aught of earthly mould,
　　Transcended thee.

In thy dark eyes a spell
　　Of beauty lingers, but their glance of fire,
When thy proud spirit is aroused, might quell
　　The lion's ire.

Thou movest floatingly,
　　As the light cloud that to the zephyr yields,
But with a step proud as a queen's might be
　　O'er conquered fields.

And thou hast that strange gift,
　　The gift of genius, high and proud and strong,
At whose behest thoughts beautiful and swift
　　Around thee throng.

They come to thee from far,
　　From air, and earth, and ocean's boundless deeps ;
They rush in glory from each shining star
　　On heaven's blue steeps.

They leap from earth's far bound—
　　Forth from the red volcano's depths they start—
From bow and cloud they float—and gather round
　　Thy burning heart.

Then at thy high command
　　They stand all marshaled in thy peerless lay,
As some great warrior marshals his proud band
　　In bright array.

Thy hand has power to trace
   Words as enduring as yon planet's flame,
Words that forever, 'mid our changing race,
   Will keep thy name.

Linked with bright song alone,
   That name o'er Time's wild heaving waves will sweep,
As o'er the water sweeps the bugle tone
   At midnight deep.

Thy magic strains will make
   A portion of earth's living music, heard
Forever, like the cadences of lake
   And breeze and bird.

The world of Nature glows
   In thy bright page more lovely to the eye,
As when, o'er hills and plain, the sunset throws
   Its golden dye.

And thou art very dear
   To many hearts, thou bright and gifted one,
Aye, men adore thee, as the Persian seer
   Adored the sun.

A MEMORY.

I KNOW a fair young girl,
   With a spirit wild and free
As the birds that flit o'er the dimpling wave,
   Then away to the wildwood flee ;
And she seems like a wreath of mist,
   As she moves through the summer bowers,
With a step too floatingly soft to break
   The sleep of the dreaming flowers.

Her eye is bright and clear
   As the depths of a shaded spring,
And beauty's name on her brow is set—
   On her cheek its signet-ring ;
And her voice is like the sound
   · Of a wave through the twilight leaves,
Or a Peri's tones from a moonlight cloud
   In the hush of the summer eves.

Along her temples pale,
   The blue veins seem to flow,
In their winding course, half seen, half hid,
   Like streams in a field of snow ;

And her shining tresses there
   Their beautiful light unfold,
Like a painted cloud where the sunset lifts
   Its shadowy wings of gold.

To me each thought of her
   Is a gleam of light and love,
A gentle dream sent down to earth
   From the holy depths above;
'T is a blessed sunbeam cast
   On affliction's cloud of tears,
A star o'er the waste of a weary heart,
   A bow on the sky of years.

THE FLIGHT OF YEARS.

GONE! gone forever!—like a rushing wave
  Another Year has burst upon the shore
Of earthly being, and its last low tones,
Wandering in broken accents on the air,
Are dying to an echo.
                    The gay Spring,
With its young charms, has gone—gone with its leaves—
Its atmosphere of roses—its white clouds
Slumbering like seraphs in the air—its birds
Telling their loves in music—and its streams
Leaping and shouting from the up-piled rocks
To make earth echo with the joy of waves.
And Summer, with its dews and showers, has gone—
Its rainbows glowing on the distant cloud
Like Spirits of the Storm—its peaceful lakes
Smiling in their sweet sleep, as if their dreams
Were of the opening flowers and budding trees
And overhanging sky—and its bright mists
Resting upon the mountain-tops, as crowns
Upon the heads of giants. Autumn, too,
Has gone, with all its deeper glories—gone

With its green hills like altars of the world
Lifting their rich fruit-offerings to their God—
Its cool winds straying mid the forest aisles
To wake their thousand wind-harps—its serene
And holy sunsets hanging o'er the West
Like banners from the battlements of heaven—
And its still evenings, when the moonlit sea
Was ever throbbing, like the living heart
Of the great Universe.   Aye—these are now
But sounds and visions of the Past—their deep,
Wild beauty has departed from the earth,
And they are gathered to the embrace of Death,
Their solemn herald to Eternity.

Nor have they gone alone.   High human hearts
Of passion have gone with them.   The fresh dust
Is chill on many a breast, that burned erewhile
With fires that seemed immortal.   Joys, that leaped
Like angels from the heart, and wandered free
In life's young morn to look upon the flowers,
The poetry of nature, and to list
The woven sounds of breeze, and bird, and stream,
Upon the night-air, have been stricken down
In silence to the dust.   Exultant Hope,
That roved forever on the buoyant winds
Like the bright, starry bird of Paradise,
And chanted to the ever-listening heart

In the wild music of a thousand tongues,
Or soared into the open sky, until
Night's burning gems seemed jeweled on her brow,
Has shut her drooping wing, and made her home
Within the voiceless sepulcher.   And Love,
That knelt at Passion's holiest shrine, and gazed
On his heart's idol as on some sweet star,
Whose purity and distance make it dear,
And dreamed of ecstacies, until his soul
Seemed but a lyre that wakened in the glance
Of the beloved one—he too has gone
To his eternal resting-place.   And where
Is stern Ambition—he who madly grasped
At Glory's fleeting phantom—he who sought
His fame upon the battlefield, and longed
To make his throne a pyramid of bones
Amid the sea of blood?   He too has gone !
His stormy voice is mute—his mighty arm
Is nerveless on its clod—his very name
Is but a meteor of the night of years
Whose gleams flashed out a moment o'er the earth,
And faded into nothingness.   The dream
Of high devotion, beauty's bright array,
And life's deep idol memories—all have passed
Like the cloud-shadows on the starlit stream,
Or a soft strain of music, when the winds

Are slumbering on the billow.
                Yet, why muse
Upon the Past with sorrow? Though the Year
Has gone to blend with the mysterious tide
Of old Eternity, and borne along
Upon its heaving breast a thousand wrecks
Of glory and of beauty—yet, why mourn
That such is destiny? Another Year
Succeedeth to the past—in their bright round
The seasons came and go—the same blue arch,
That hath hung o'er us, will hang o'er us yet—
The same pure stars that we have loved to watch,
Will blossom still at twilight's gentle hour
Like lilies on the tomb of Day—and still
Man will remain, to dream as he hath dreamed,
And mark the earth with passion. Love will spring
From the lone tomb of old affections—Hope
And Joy and great Ambition, will rise up
As they have risen—and their deeds will be
Brighter than those engraven on the scroll
Of parted centuries. Even now the sea
Of coming years, beneath whose mighty waves
Life's great events are heaving into birth,
Is tossing to and fro, as if the winds
Of heaven were prisoned in its soundless depths
And struggling to be free.

Weep not, that Time
Is passing on—it will ere long reveal
A brighter era to the nations.   Hark !
Along the vales and mountains of the earth
There is a deep, portentous murmuring,
Like the swift rush of subterranean streams,
Or like the mingled sounds of earth and air,
When the fierce Tempest, with sonorous wing,
Heaves his deep folds upon the rushing winds,
And hurries onward with his night of clouds
Against the eternal mountains.   'T is the voice
Of infant Freedom—and her stirring call
Is heard and answered in a thousand tones
From every hill-top of her Western home ;
And lo ! it breaks across old Ocean's flood,
And " Freedom ! Freedom !" is the answering shout
Of nations starting from the spell of years.
The day-spring !—see, 't is brightening in the heavens !
The watchmen of the night have caught the sign—
From tower to tower the signal-fires flash free—
And the deep watch-word, like the rush of seas
That heralds the volcano's bursting flame,
Is sounding o'er the earth.   Bright years of hope
And life are on the wing !—yon glorious bow
Of Freedom, bended by the hand of God,
Is spanning Time's dark surges.   Its high arch,
A type of Love and Mercy on the cloud,

Tells that the many storms of human life
Will pass in silence, and the sinking waves,
Gathering the forms of glory and of peace,
Reflect the undimmed brightness of the heavens.

TO A BEAUTIFUL AUTHORESS.*

I LONGED to see thee, gifted one,
   For fame, in accents warm,
Had told me of thy loveliness
Of mind, and face, and form ;
But oh, I did not think to meet
Such charms as I have met ;
My dreams of thee were very bright,
But thou art brighter yet.

When Plato lay, in infancy,
In slumber's soft eclipse,
'T is said the gentle honey-bees
Came clustering 'round his lips ;
And thus, as on thy lips we look,
So eloquent and warm,
A thousand sweet and wingéd thoughts
Around thee seem to swarm.

* The authoress of " Belle Smith Abroad."

A spell is in thy dark, bright eyes,
The wildest soul to tame,
Dark as the tempest-cloud and bright
As its quick glance of flame;
And gazing in their earnest depths,
I see more angels there
Than fancy, to a dreaming seer,
E'er pictured in the air.

Young Genius his own coronal
Around thy forehead wreathes,
And high thoughts are the atmosphere
In which thy spirit breathes;
Thy soul can read the mysteries
Of cloud, and sky, and star,
And hear the tones of Eden-spheres
Borne sweetly down from far.

For thee, the soul of poetry
The universe pervades—
It glitters in the light, and dwells,
All softened, in the shades;
The young waves murmur it, the dew
Reflects it from the flower,
The blue skies breathe it, and the air
Thrills with its mystic power.

Press on, bright one, press proudly on
To win the laurel crown,
And set thy living name among
The names of old renown ;
Press on, press on, and thy bright fame
Will never, never die,
But, like the ivy, brighter grow
As centuries pass by.

HENRY CLAY.

[WRITTEN AFTER HIS DEATH.]

WITH voice and mien of stern control,
 He stood among the great and proud,
And words of fire burst from his soul
 Like lightnings from the tempest-cloud ;
His high and deathless themes were crowned
 With glory of his genius born,
And gloom and ruin darkly frowned
 Where fell his bolts of wrath and scorn.

But he is gone, the free, the bold,
 The champion of his country's right ;
His burning eye is dim and cold,
 And mute his voice of conscious might.
Oh, no ! not mute ; the stirring call
 Can startle tyrants on their thrones,
And on the hearts of nations fall
 More awful than his living tones.

The impulse that his spirit gave
  To human thought's wild, stormy sea,
Will heave and thrill through every wave
  Of that great deep eternally;
And the all-circling atmosphere,
  With which is blent his breath of flame,
Will sound with cadence deep and clear,
  In storm and calm, his voice and name.

His words, that like a bugle blast
  Erst rang along the Grecian shore,
And o'er the hoary Andes passed,
  Will still ring on forevermore.
Great Liberty will catch the sounds,
  And start to newer, brighter life,
And summon from earth's utmost bounds
  Her children to the glorious strife.

Unnumbered pilgrims o'er the wave,
  In the far ages yet to be,
Will come to kneel beside his grave,
  And hail him prophet of the free.
'Tis holier ground, that lowly bed,
  In which his mouldering form is laid,
Than fields where Liberty has bled
  Beside her broken battle-blade.

Who, now in danger's fearful hour,
　　When all around is wild and dark,
Shall guide, with voice and arm of power,
　　Our Freedom's consecrated ark?
With stricken hearts, O God! to thee,
　　Beneath whose feet the stars are dust,
We bow, and ask that thou wilt be,
　　Through every ill, our stay and trust.

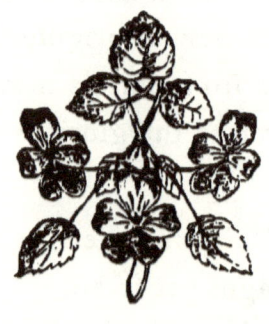

MY OLD HOME.

AND I have come yet once again to stray
Where erst I strayed in childhood. Oh, 'tis sweet
To gaze upon the dear old landscape! Here
My thoughts first reveled in the wild delight
Of new existence! Here my infant eye
First dwelt on Nature in her loveliness:
The golden flash of waters, the bright flowers
That seemed to spring in very wantonness
From every hill and stream; the earth's green leaves,
The moonlight mountains, the bright crimson gush,
That deepening streamed along the skies of morn,
And the rich heavens of sunset! Here I loved
To gaze upon the holy arch of eve
In breathless longing, till I almost dreamed
That I was mingling with its glorious depths,
A portion of their purity; to muse
Upon the stars through many a lonely night,
Till their deep tones of mystic minstrelsy
Were borne into my heart; to list at morn
The gentle voice of song-birds in their joy
Lifting on high their matins, till my soul,

Like theirs, gushed forth in music; and to look
Upon the clouds in beauty wandering up
The deep blue zenith, till my heart, like them,
Went far away through yon high paths to seek
The home of thought and spirit in the heavens.

———

YEARS have passed by upon their shadowy wings,
Yet o'er this spot no change has come to tell
The noiseless flight of Time.   The far-off hills
Are still as blue, the wave as musical,
The wild rose blooms as fresh and fair, the winds
Breathe yet as freshly on my brow, the trees
Still cast as soft a shadow, and as sweet
The violet springs to woo the breath of heaven,
As in my years of infancy.   I range
Where erst I sported by the leaping stream,
And the glad birds, as they remembered yet
And loved the stranger, chant the same sweet songs
I strayed to hear ere childhood's silken locks
Had darkened on my temples.   Can it be
That the dark seal of Time and Change is set
Upon my brow? Each spot I loved still blooms
In beauty undecayed; I hear no sound
That tells the tale of years; and can it be
That I alone am faded? Were it not

That many a fearful tale of sin and woe,
And strife and desolation, has been graved
On Memory's darkened scroll—oh, were it not
That passion's burning pathway has been traced
So deep, so fiercely vivid, that my heart
Is withering yet beneath it, I could deem
That I were still a pure and sinless child
Just 'wakened from a long, long dream of tears,
To gaze again in infant recklessness
On earth, and heaven, and ocean, and again
To paint the future as a lovely throng
Of bright and glorious visions beckoning on
To the blue beauty of life's Eden-isles.

———

AH! 'tis as in my childhood.   Years have passed,
Long years of weariness, since last I gazed
Upon those hills and waters ; yet again,
As here I muse, life's early memories
Steal in their freshness o'er me, and my heart
Leaps to the sweet, wild melody that thrilled
Through all its depths ere life's bright bow had gone
From childhood's purple morning, or the stream
Of Time, that gushed exulting by, had lost
The tints of Heaven's blue beauty.   Memory hangs
With fondness on each dear memento yet,

That tells of those far years ; and many a chord,
Touched by her melancholy hand, awakes
From its long, dreamless slumber, and its strains
Of sweet and mournful music faintly fall
Upon the ear of Fancy, like the tones
That come upon the dying winds of eve
From the far moonlight ocean, when the storm
Sleeps on the night-cloud and the waters heave
As heaves the stricken bosom.

                        Every scene
Is living with the voiceless spirit still
Of life's departed Eden.   Early joys,
So sweet, so beautiful, they almost seem
The wild creations of a wizard tale,
With lightning-glow are flashing up life's stream,
And breaking on my spirit with a power
I thought had died to live no more.   I gaze
On scenes once blended with the happy hours
Of youth and ecstasy, and feel that life,
Though shadowed by the somber wing of years,
Is not all turned to bitterness.   The flame
Has fallen, and its high and fitful gleams
Perchance have faded, but the living fires
Still glow beneath the ashes. 'The bright stream
Is wasted, and its wave has ceased to flash
In gladness to the sunlight, and to bear
The flowers upon its sparkling bosom, yet

'T will flow on in undying freshness still
Deep in its buried channels evermore.

———

Ah! how the silent memories of years
Are stirring in my spirit. I have been
A lone and joyless wanderer. I have roamed
Abroad through other climes, where tropic flowers
Were offering up their incense, and the stars
Swimming like living creatures; I have strayed
Where the soft skies of Italy were hung
In beautiful transparency above,
And glory floating like a lovely dream
O'er the rich landscape; yet dear Fancy still,
'Mid all the richer glow of brighter realms,
Oft turned to picture the remembered home,
That blessed its earliest day-dreams. Must I go
Forth in the world again? I've proved its joys,
Till joy was turned to bitterness—I've felt
Its sorrows till I thought my heart would burst
With the fierce rush of tears! The sorrowing babe
Clings to its mother's breast. The bleeding dove
Flies to her native vale, and nestles there
To die amid the quiet grove, where first
She tried her tender pinion. I could love
Thus to repose amid these peaceful scenes

To memory dear. Oh, it were passing sweet
To rest forever on this lovely spot,
Where passed my days of innocence—to dream
Of the pure stream of infant happiness
Sunk in life's wild and burning sands—to dwell
On visions faded, till my broken heart
Should cease to throb—to purify my soul
With high and holy musings—and to lift
Its aspirations to the central home
Of love, and peace, and holiness in Heaven.

NIGHT IN CAVE HILL CEMETERY.

ONE evening, dear Virginia, in thy life,
  When thou and I were straying side by side
Beneath the holy moonlight, and our thoughts
Seemed taking a deep hue of mournfulness
From the sweet, solemn hour, I said—if thou,
Whose young years scarcely numbered half my own,
Should'st pass before me to the spirit-land,
I would, on some mild eve beneath the moon,
Shining in heaven as it was shining then,
Go forth alone to lay me by thy grave,
And render to thy cherished memory
The last sad tribute of a stricken heart.
Thine answer was a sigh, a tear, a sob,
A gentle pressure of the hand, and thus
My earnest vow was hallowed. A thin cloud,
Like a pale winding-sheet, that moment passed
Across the moon, and as its shadow fell,
Like a mysterious omen of the tomb,
Upon our kindred spirits, thou didst turn
Thine eye to that wan specter of the skies,
And, gazing on the solemn portent, weep
As if thy head were waters.

                  Weary years
Since then have planted furrows on my brow,
And sorrows in my heart, and the pale moon,
That shone around us on that lovely eve,
Is shining now upon thy swarded grave,
And I have come, a pilgrim of the night,
To bow at Memory's holy shrine, and keep
My unforgotten vow.
               Dear, parted one,
Friend of my better years, dark months have passed
With all their awful shadows o'er the earth,
Since the green turf was laid above thy rest,
'Mid sighs and streaming tears and stifled groans,
But, oh ! thy gentle memory is not dim
In the deep hearts that loved thee.   We have set
This sweet young rose-tree o'er thy hallowed grave,
And may the skies shed their serenest dews
Around it, may the summer clouds distil
Their gentlest rains upon it, may the fresh
Warm zephyrs fan it with their softest breath,
And daily may the bright and holy beams
Of morning greet it with their sweetest smile,
That it may wave its roses o'er thy dust,
Dear emblems of the flowers that thou so oft
In life didst fling.upon our happy hearts
From thy own spirit's Eden.   Yet we know

'T is but an humble offering to thee,
Who dwellest where the fadeless roses bloom,
In Heaven's eternal sunshine.
                              To our eyes
Thy beauty has not faded from the earth ;
We see it in the flowers that lift their lids
To greet the early spring-time, in the bow
The magic pencil of the sunshine paints
Upon the flying rain-clouds, in the stars
That glitter from the blue abyss of night,
And in the strange, mysterious loveliness
Of every holy sunset.   To our ears
The music of thy loved tones is not lost ;
We hear it in the low, sweet cadences
Of wave and stream and fountain, in the notes
Of birds that from the sky and forest hail
The sunrise with their songs, and in the wild
And soul-like breathings of the evening wind
Of grove and forest.   Yet no sight or sound
In all the world of Nature is as sweet,
Dear, lost Virginia, as when thou wast here
To gaze and listen with us.   The young flowers
And the pure stars seem pale and cold and dim,
As if they looked through blinding tears :—alas !
The tears are in our eyes.   The melodies
Of wave and stream and bird and forest-harp,

Borne on the soft wings of the evening gale,
Seem blended with a deep wail for the dead :—
Alas ! the wail is in our hearts.

                  Lost one !
We miss thee in our sadness and our joy !
When at the solemn eventide we stray,
'Mid the still gathering of the twilight shades,
To muse upon the dear and hallowed Past,
With its deep, mournful memories, a voice
Comes from the still recesses of our hearts—
" *She is not here !*"   In the gay, festive hour,
When music peals upon the perfumed air,
And wit and mirth are ringing in our ears,
And light forms floating round us in the dance,
And jewels flashing through luxuriant curls,
And deep tones breathing vows of tenderness
And truth to listening beauty, even·then,
Amid the wild enchantments of the hour,
To many a heart the Past comes back again,
And, as the fountain of its tears is stirred,
A voice comes sounding from its holiest depths—
" *Alas ! she is not here !*"   The spring-time now
Is forth upon the fresh green earth, the vales
Are one bright wilderness of blooms, the woods,
With all their wealth of rainbow tints, repose,
Like fairy clouds upon the vernal sky,

And every gale is burdened with the gush
Of music—free, wild music ; yet, lost one,
Through all these wildering melodies, that voice
As from the very heart of Nature comes—
"Alas! she is not here!" But list! oh, list!—
From the eternal depths of yonder sky,
From where the flash of sun and star is dim,
Is uncreated light, an angel strain,
As sweet as that in which the morning stars
Together sang o'er the creation's birth,
Comes floating downward through the ravished air—
"Joy! joy! she's here! she's here!"
                        'T is midnight deep,
And a pale cloud, like that whose shadow fell
Upon our souls on that remembered eve,
Is passing o'er the moon, but now the shade
Falls on one heart alone.   I am alone,
My dear and long-lost friend.   Oh! wheresoe'er
In the vast universe of God thou art,
I pray thee stoop at this mysterious hour
To the dark earth from thy all-radiant home,
And hold communion with thy weeping friend
As in the hours departed.
                  Ah, I feel,
Sweet spirit, thou hast heard and blessed my prayer !
I hear the rustling of thy angel-plumes

About me and around ; the very air
Is glowing with a thousand seraph thoughts,
Bright as the sparkles of a shooting star ;
A hand, from which the electric fire of Heaven
Seems flashing through my frame, is clasped in mine ;
Thy blessed voice, with its remembered tones
Softened to more than mortal melody,
Is thrilling through my heart, as 't were the voice
Of the lost Pleiad calling from its place
In the eternal void ; and our two souls
Blend once again as erst they used to blend
The heavenly with the earthly !
                        Fare thee well !
Sweet spirit, fare thee well ! The blessed words
That thou, this night, hast whispered to me here,
Above the mound that hides thy mortal form,
Will purify my soul and strengthen me
To bear the ills and agonies of life,
And point me to an immortality
With thee in God's own holy Paradise.

TO MISS SALLIE M. BRYAN.

LONG thy mystic tones, dear Sallie,
 Have been sounding through my brain,
Like the distant voice of ocean,
 In the pause of wind and rain ;
And in midnight's solemn musings,
 And the haunted dreams of sleep,
Oft to thine my spirit answers,
 As deep calleth unto deep.

I have dreamed thy soul a sea-shell,
 From the upper deep sublime,
Cast by some unpitying billow
 On this rocky shore of Time,
Where its sweet and dirge-like breathings
 Seems a low and mournful sigh—
A deep, ever restless pining
 For its far home in the sky.

I have dreamed thy soul a wind-harp,
 Of a weird and wondrous power,
Breathing out its strange, wild music,
 In the twilight's wizard-hour,

Gently swept by gales of Eden,
  (When the earth-wind's wings are furled),
And in mournful cadence telling
  Of its own dear native world.

There's a realm within thy spirit,
  Filled with grandeur and with gloom,
Where each tone is like a heart-wail,
  And each earth-swell seems a tomb;
And the flowers—a somber tinting
  Overspreads their ghastly forms,
As if nurtured by the droppings
  But of passing thunder-storms.

While thy calm, angelic features
  In serenest beauty sleep,
Thy high thoughts, in vivid flashes,
  On our startled vision leap :—
'T is as if the keen, red lightning
  Should burst wildly from the fold
Of a soft, white cloud of morning
  Tinged with violet, blue and gold.

There's a tall plant of the tropics,
  That, amid its bristling spears,
Puts forth one all-beauteous blossom
  With each score of passing years;

And our human race, dear minstrel,
    Is a plant of kindred power :—
Once in each score years it blossoms,
    And thou art its glorious flower.

FANNIE.

DEAR FANNIE, in the twilight sweet,
  I've mused upon the long-gone hours,
When, touched by your light, fairy feet,
    My path grew red and white with flowers.
Together oft we loved to stray,
    And sometimes by my side you stood,
But oftener chose to bound away
    In girlhood's wild and frolic mood.
And I, at such times, used to sit
    And watch you flitting o'er the plain
As light as troops of fairies flit
    Across the poet's dreaming brain.
Your voice was music to my soul—
    It seemed the cadence of the dove ;
And oft we talked, without control,
    On every earthly theme but love.
Ah, *that* was never said or sung
    Where we in gentle converse tarried,
For, Fannie, you were very young,
    And I—was elderly and married.

We were not more unlike in years
   Than thoughts and feelings. I was staid,
And you a child of smiles and tears,
   A wild and self-willed little maid.
I crownéd you May Queen once, and swore
   Allegiance till the May-day's close,
But, ere the next half-hour was o'er,
   I beat you with a full-blown rose.
Then I the blooming missile sent
   Right at your laughing cheek and missed you,
And then, as graver punishment,
   I caught you in my arms and kissed you.
Full at my head your crown you threw,
   In all its wealth and vernal splendor,
Then, frightened, to your feet I flew
   And knelt, a penitent offender.
We verged, at times on quarrel's brink,
   We matched keen wits at every meeting,
But you ne'er had from me, I think,
   But that one kiss and that one beating.

A sad, sad parting came at last :
   You roamed afar—I scarce knew why ;
From out my path a sweet flower passed,
   A bright star wandered from my sky.
I did not dream to see you more,
   Or listen to your cadence sweet,

But here, upon this Southern shore,
   Again for one brief hour we meet.
The scent of flower, the note of bird,
   Are loading this delicious breeze,
But your dear face and voice have stirred
   My spirit's depths far more than these.
Ah, Fannie, you are young and bright,
   And lovers, by the dozen, throng
Forever round you, day and night,
   With wit, and blandishment, and song ;
But, well I know, my darling pet,
   You do not let such trifles trouble you,
Your wild heart is unconquered yet—
   Is it not so, dear Fannie W. ?

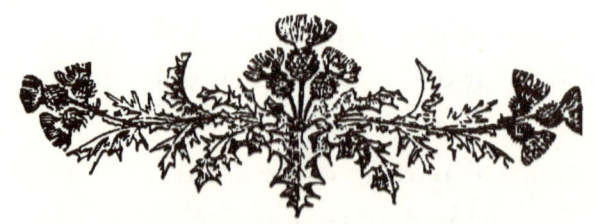

A FAREWELL.

I MET thee in a stranger land
   Far from my own blue streams,
And gloriously the vision shone
   Upon my spirit's dreams;
And then my lyre, that long had slept
Unvisited, unheard, unswept,
   Awoke in Beauty's gleams,
As erst the harp of Memnon woke
When o'er its chords the morning broke.

We met, and soon my spirit bowed,
   Unshadowed girl, to thee,
As the bright bow upon the cloud
   Bends to the monarch-sea.
Thy words, thy tones, the smiles that played
Upon thy lovely features, bade
   Long-hidden thoughts go free;
And sweetly in my manhood's tears
Were glassed the tints of earlier years.

And now we part—these simple words
　May be my last farewell,
But often o'er my bosom's chords
　Thy spirit-tones will swell;
The happy hours since first we met
Upon my heart and life have set
　A deep and deathless spell;
And thou wilt be, although afar,
Of memory's heaven the dearest star.

Farewell! farewell! yon moon is bright
　And calm and pure like thee;
But, lo! a dark cloud dims its light—
　The type, alas, of me;
From the blue heavens the cloud will go,
But the unfading moon will glow
　Still beautiful and free;
And thus thy life with fadeless ray
Will shine when I am passed away.

YOUNG ADELAIDE.

WHEN Morn comes, beautiful and calm,
 With cheek of bloom and breath of balm,
And stoops o'er rose and violet blue
To kiss them with her lips of dew,
And bids the waves and breezes wake
Their fairy tones on stream and lake,
I love to stray o'er hill and glade
And think of thee, young Adelaide.

And when the birds at evening fold
Their glancing wings of blue and gold,
And white mists in the starlight shine,
Floating with motion soft as thine,
And Night in her strange beauty vies
With thy dark hair and starry eyes,
I love to stray o'er vale and lea,
And think, young Adelaide, of thee.

A NIGHT SCENE.

'TIS a sweet scene. 'Mid shadows dim
   The mighty river wanders by,
And on its calm, unruffled brim,
   So soft the bright star-shadows lie,
'T would seem as if the night-wind's plume
Had swept through woods of tropic bloom,
And shaken down their blossoms white
To float upon the waves to-night.

And see ! as soars the moon aloft,
   Her yellow beams come through the air
So mild, so beautifully soft,
   That wave and wood seem stirred with prayer :
And the pure spirit, as it kneels
At Nature's holy altar, feels
Religion's self come stealing by
In every beam that cleaves the sky.

The living soul of beauty fills
   The air with glorious visions : bright
They wander o'er the forest hills
   And linger in the pallid light ;

Off to the breathing heavens they go,
Along the earth they live and glow,
Shed on the stream their holy smiles,
And beckon to its purple isles.

RAPHAEL TO JULIA.

THOU gav'st thy hand, all trembling like a dove,
  To one who deemed thee, as thou art, divine,
But could *he* love thee with the glorious love
  That's due to such a fiery heart as thine?

Thou wast to him the idol of his years,
  A star to light his pathway from on high,
But could *his* soul dissolve in love and tears,
  Or soar with thine into the broad, blue sky?

When thy keen spirit on its wing of fire
  Rose proudly up above our mortal state,
To list the music of the starry lyre,
  Did'st thou not sigh for some high spirit-mate?

Oh, my heart's idol! could thy bosom proud
  Give back the wild and burning love of mine,
Our souls should mate like eagles in the cloud
  Where the storm welters and its rainbows shine!

I could defy pain, death, my soul's unrest,
  In the fierce struggle for such glorious prize—
What could I fear, while clasping to my breast
  All that I know or dream of Paradise?

THE PARTING.

THE signal from the distant strand
   Streams o'er the waters blue—
It bids me press thy parting hand,
   And breathe my last adieu;
But oft on fancy's glowing wing
   My heart will love to stray,
And still to thee with rapture spring,
   Though I am far away.

With thee I've wandered oft to hear,
   On Summer's quiet eves,
The wild-bird's music, soft and clear,
   Borne through the whispering leaves,
Or see the moon's bright shadow laid
   Upon the waveless bay:
Those eves—their memory can not fade,
   Though I am far away.

My life may feel Hope's withering blight,
   Yet Fancy's tearful eye
Will turn to thee—the dearest light
   In retrospection's sky;

And still the memory of our love,
　While life was young and gay,
Will sweetly o'er my spirit move,
　Though I am far away.

'T is hard, when Spring's first flower expands,
　To pass it coldly by,
Or see upon the desert sands
　The gem unheeded lie ;
The gentle thoughts that bless the hours
　Of love can ne'er decay,
And thou wilt live in memory's bowers,
　Though I am far away.

The sun has sunk, with fading gleam,
　Down evening's shadowy vale,
But see—his softened glories stream
　From yonder crescent pale ;
And thus affection's chastened light
　Will memory still display,
To gild the gloom of sorrow's night,
　Though I am far away.

LILY MERRILL.

I 'VE looked on many a lovely face
    In cold New England's stormy clime,
I 've knelt to woman's floating grace
    Beneath the orange and the lime ;
I 've heard, through all our mighty land,
    Her soft tones thrill upon the air,
And sometimes dared to bathe my hand
    Amid the bright waves of her hair ;
I 've lingered oft in hall and bower,
    But still my heart and life seemed sterile,
Until they burst to glorious flower
    Beneath the smile of Lily Merrill.

In Italy I oft have strayed
    Where love and mirth and beauty shine ;
I 've looked on many a Georgian maid,
    Whose beauty almost seemed divine ;
I 've dwelt beneath the skies of Spain,
    Within the old white walls of Cadiz,

And listened to love's melting strain
　　Breathed o'er the lutes of Spanish ladies ;
But ah, I never, never felt
　　My wandering heart in mortal peril,
Until in ecstasy I knelt
　　To the young charms of Lily Merrill

I met her in the joyous dance,
　　Where music's soft and thrilling strain
Swelled on the air, and every glance
　　Fixed her sweet image on my brain ;
I saw her move in pride of power,
　　'Mid beauty's bright, bewitching daughters,
As graceful as her namesake flower
　　Upon the blue lake's heaving waters ;
Amid her free and lovely tresses
　　She wore no diamond, pearl, or beryl,
But oft my heart with rapture blesses
　　The night I met young Lily Merrill.

TO MARIAN PRENTICE PIATT:

AN INFANT.

CHILD of two poets, whose rich songs
  Have won a high and peerless fame,
I thank them, that to thee belongs
  A portion of my humble name—
That they have blent for thee its tone
With the sweet music of their own.

As yet, dear child, thou hast not trod
  The paths of life where grief is met,
But beauty, like a smile of God,
  Upon thy little brow is set ;
And, oh ! may Heaven forever bless
Thy life with love and happiness.

A germ of genius, high and good,
  Methinks within thy bosom lies,
Which, in thy coming womanhood,
  Will bear bright blossoms for the skies—
Aye, bear even in these earthly bowers
Eternity's all-glorious flowers.

May all thy life a poem be,
    Oh, sweet as e'er thy mother writ,
And beauteous as the visions fair   ·
    That through thy father's spirit flit ;
And may that poem, bright and high,
Be set to music of the sky.

THE DEATH-DAY OF WILLIAM COURTLAND PRENTICE.

ONCE more I come at set of sun
   To sit beside thee, long-lost one ;
To muse upon thy joyous prime,
In that dear, unforgotten time
When thou didst bound o'er hills and plains,
Life running wild in all thy veins,
And thou in manhood's young estate
Didst almost seem to challenge fate.

Thine eagle-spirit ever soared
Where thunders broke and tempests roared—
Through battle's flame and smoke it dashed
Where bayonets gleamed and sabres clashed ;
But ah, a fatal shaft was sped,
And thou wast with the stricken dead ;—
Now thou art here beneath these clods,
Struck by man's lightning, not by God's.

Dear Courtland, thou, the strong, the brave,
Fillest a warrior's bloody grave ;
The soil above thee, wet with showers,
Gives birth to sweet and beauteous flowers ;
But e'en the white rose to my view
Bears in its veins a crimson hue,
As if its mournful essence came
From the red death-wounds of thy frame.

Thou sleepest well !   The bugle-note
Of battle may above thee float ;
The tramp of charging hosts around
May like an earthquake shake the ground ;
The cannon's voice, the victors' shout,
May through the sulphurous air peal out ;
But thou wilt sleep amid the roar—
No power but God's can wake thee more.

Perchance, when fallen in the strife,
Thy young lips breathed a prayer for life ;
Perchance thy heart heaved one deep sigh
To think that thou so soon must die.
But, had it been thy lot to know
The coming triumph of thy foe ;
Hadst thou foreseen, all rent and riven,
The cause to which thy soul was given ;
Foreseen the flag, thy guide, thy star,

Trailed low behind the conqueror's car;
Foreseen fierce desolation stride
O'er the bright land that was thy pride;
Foreseen hill, plain, and vale, and wood,
Swept as by storms of fire and blood:
The clime where Heaven's best blessings fell
Changed by man's passions to a hell:
Its homes, where joy and love erst met,
By hunger's howling wolves beset:
Its human forms like skeletons,
Its streams like ghostly Phlegethons—
Thou would'st have blessed with latest breath
A kind God for his angel, Death.

Thy form is in this sacred spot,
Thy memory and thy soul are not;
Thy name high hearts will love to keep
Through all thy lone and solemn sleep.
Oft bards have strung and bards will string
Their sweet and holy lyres to fling
Pure song-wreaths, evermore to bloom
Like amaranths upon thy tomb;
And thoughts of thee in deep souls lie
Like golden clouds in Autumn's sky.
Bright ones will sigh—the young, the old—
When thy young destiny is told;

Thy laurels, with soft heart-dews wet,
Brighten as suns shall rise and set,
And tear-founts heave and swell to thee,
As to yon moon the heaving sea.

ELEGIAC.*

HERE, whilst the twilight dews
　　Are softly gathering on the leaves and flowers,
　I come, oh patriot dead, to muse
　　　A few brief hours.

　　Hard by you, rank on rank,
　Rise the sad evergreens, whose solemn forms
　　Are dark as if they only drank
　　　The thunder storms.

　　Through the thick leaves around
　The low, wild winds their dirge-like music pour,
　　Like the far ocean's solemn sound
　　　On its lone shore.

　　From all the air a sigh,
　Dirge-like, and soul-like, melancholy, wild,
　　Comes like a mother's wailing cry
　　　O'er her dead child.

* Written in the portion of Cave Hill Cemetery, Louisville,
allotted to the Union Dead.

Yonder, a little way,
Where mounds rise thick like surges on the sea,
Those whom ye met in fierce array
Sleep dreamlessly.

The same soft breezes sing,
The same birds chant their spirit-requiem,
The same sad flowers their fragrance fling
O'er you and them.

And pilgrims oft will grieve
Alike o'er Northern and o'er Southern dust,
And both to God's great mercy leave
In equal trust.

Oh, ye and they, as foes,
Will meet no more, but calmly take your rest,
The meek hands folded in repose
On each still breast.

No marble columns rear
Their shafts to blazon each dead hero's name,
Yet well, oh well, ye slumber here,
Great sons of fame!

The dead as free will start
From the unburdened as the burdened sod,
And stand as pure in soul and heart
Before their God.

*   *   *   *   *   *

'T is morn—as lone I stand,
The dawn is reddening o'er each humble grave ;
Oh, when shall night pass from the land
Ye die to save?

Through all the upper air
May your life-blood in exhalations rise,
A ghastly cloud of red despair
To traitor eyes.

And may the lightnings dire,
Coiled in that cloud, like vengeful scorpions dart
To blast with their keen fangs of fire
Each traitor heart.

LINES

TO ALICE M'CLURE GRIFFIN.

I THINK of thee when Eastern skies
  Are gleaming with the dawn's first red—
Of thee when sunset's fairy dyes
  In beauty o'er the West are shed ;
My thoughts are thine mid toil and strife,
  Thine when all care and sorrow flee,
Aye thine, forever thine ;—my life
  Is but a living thought of thee.

I think of thee when Spring's first flowers
  O'er hill and plain and valley glow—
Of thee, mid Autumn's purple bowers,
  And cold December's wastes of snow.
My thoughts are thine when joys depart,
  Thine when from weary trouble free,
Aye, thine, forever thine ;—my heart
  Is but a throbbing thought of thee.

LOOKOUT MOUNTAIN.

HISTORIC MOUNT! baptized in flame and blood,
    Thy name is as immortal as the rocks
That crown thy thunder-scarred but royal brow.
Thou liftest up thy aged head in pride
In the cool atmosphere, but higher still
Within the calm and solemn atmosphere
Of an immortal fame.   From thy sublime
And awful summit, I can gaze afar
Upon innumerous lesser pinnacles,
And oh! my wingéd spirit loves to fly,
Like a strong eagle, 'mid their up-piled crags.
But most on thee, imperial mount, my soul
Is chained as by a spell of power.
                              I gaze
From this tall height on Chickamauga's field,
Where Death held erst high carnival. · The waves
Of the mysterious death-river moaned;
The tramp, the shout, the fearful thunder-roar
Of red-breath'd cannon, and the wailing cry

Of myriad victims, filled the air.   The smoke
Of battle closed above the charging hosts,
And, when it passed, the grand old flag no more
Waved in the light of heaven.   The soil was wet
And miry with the life-blood of the brave,
As with a drenching rain ; and yon broad stream,
The noble and majestic Tennessee,
Ran reddened toward the deep.
                         But thou, O bleak
And rocky mountain, wast the theater
Of a yet fiercer struggle.   On thy height,
Where now I sit, a proud and gallant host,
The chivalry and glory of the South,
Stood up awaiting battle.   Somber clouds,
Floating far, far beneath them, shut from view
The stern and silent foe, whose storied flag
Bore on its folds our country's monarch-bird,
Whose talons grasp the thunderbolt.   Up, up
Thy rugged sides they came with measured tramp,
Unheralded by bugle, drum, or shout,
And, though the clouds closed round them with the gloom
Of double night, they paused not in their march
Till sword and plume and bayonet emerged
Above the spectral shades that circled round
Thy awful breast.   Then suddenly a storm
Of flame and lead and iron downward burst,
From this tall pinnacle, like winter hail.

Long, fierce, and bloody was the strife—alas!
The noble flag, our country's hope and pride,
Sank down beneath the surface of the clouds,
As sinks the pennon of a shipwrecked bark
Beneath a stormy sea, and naught was heard
Save the wild cries and moans of stricken men,
And the swift rush of fleeing warriors down
Thy rugged steeps.
         But soon the trumpet-voice
Of the bold chieftain of the routed host
Resounded through the atmosphere, and pierced
The clouds that hung around thee.   With high words
He quickly summoned his brave soldiery back
To the renewal of the deadly fight;
Again their stern and measured tramp was heard
By the flushed Southrons, as it echoed up
Thy bald, majestic cliffs.   Again they burst,
Like spirits of destruction, through the clouds,
And mid a thousand hurtling missiles swept
Their foes before them as the whirlwind sweeps
The strong oaks of the forest.   Victory
Perched with her sister-eagle on the scorched
And torn and blackened banner.
         Awful mount:
The stains of blood have faded from thy rocks,
The cries of mortal agony have ceased
To echo from thy hollow cliffs, the smoke

Of battle long since melted into air,
And yet thou art unchanged.   Aye, thou wilt lift
In majesty thy walls above the storm,
Mocking the generations as they pass,
And pilgrims of the far-off centuries
Will sometimes linger in their wanderings,
To ponder, with a deep and sacred awe,
The legend of the fight above the clouds.

TO A POLITICAL OPPONENT.*

I SEND thee, Greeley, words of cheer,
  Thou bravest, truest, best of men ;
For I have marked thy strong career,
  As traced by thy own sturdy pen.
I've seen thy struggles with the foes
  That dared thee to the desperate fight,
And loved to watch thy goodly blows,
  Dealt for the cause thou deem'st the right.

Thou'st dared to stand against the wrong
  When many faltered by thy side ;
In thy own strength hast dared be strong,
  Nor on another's arm relied.
Thy own bold thoughts thou'st dared to think,
  Thy own great purposes avowed ;
And none have ever seen thee shrink
  From the fierce surges of the crowd.

    * Horace Greeley.

Thou, all unaided and aloné,
  Didst take thy way in life's young years,
With no kind hand clasped in thy own,
  No gentle voice to soothe thy fears.
But thy high heart no power could tame,
  And thou hast never ceased to feel
Within thy veins a sacred flame
  That turned thy iron nerves to steel.

I know that thou art not exempt
  From all the weaknesses of earth ;
For passion comes to rouse and tempt
  The truest souls of mortal birth.
But thou hast well fulfilled thy trust,
  In spite of love and hope and fear ;
And even the tempest's thunder-gust
  But clears thy spirit's atmosphere.

Thou still art in thy manhood's prime,
  Still foremost 'mid thy fellow-men,
Though in each year of all thy time
  Thou hast compressed three-score and ten.
· Oh, may each blessed sympathy,
  Breathed on thee with a tear and sigh,
A sweet flower in thy pathway be,
  A bright star in thy clear blue sky.

ON A BOOK OF VERSES.

TO ALICE M'CLURE GRIFFIN.

DEAR ALICE, for two happy hours,
 I've sat within this little nook
To muse upon the sweet soul-flowers
 That blossom in thy gentle book.
They lift their white and spotless bells,
 Untouched by frost, unchanged by time,
For they are blessed immortelles
 Transplanted from the Eden clime.

With pure and deep idolatry
 Upon each lovely page I've dwelt,
Till to thy spirit's sorcery
 My spirit has with reverence knelt.
Oh, every thought of thine to me
 Is like a fount, a bird, a star,
A tone of holy minstrelsy
 Down floating from the clouds afar.

The fairies have around thee traced
 A circle bright, a magic sphere—

The home of genius, beauty, taste,
　　The joyous smile, the tender tear.
　　Within that circle, calm and clear,
With Nature's softest dews impearled,
　　I sit and list, with pitying ear,
The tumults of the far-off world.

Thy book is shut; its flowers remain,
　　'Mid this mysterious twilight gloom,
Deep-imaged on my heart and brain,
　　And shed their fragrance through my room.
　　Ah, how I love their holy bloom,
As in these moonbeams, dim and wan,
　　They seem pale blossoms o'er a tomb
That 's closed upon the loved and gone.

Young angel of my waning years,*
　　Consoler of life's stormiest day,
Magician of my hopes and fears,
　　Guide of my dark and troubled way,
　　To thee this little votive lay,
In gratitude I dedicate ;
　　And with an earnest spirit pray
God's blessing on thy mortal state.

---

* At Mr. Griffin's house in Louisville, after his own home was broken up, Mr. Prentice was treated with filial tenderness by both Mr. and Mrs. Griffin.

VIOLETS.

ACCEPT, my friend, these violets blue,
    Once wet with morning's silver dew,
Now fading mournfully away,
Yet lovely still in their decay.
Young nurselings of a Southern land,
They came from gentle beauty's hand,
And I will send them now to rest
On gentler beauty's angel breast.

And there, oh, dear one ! let them sleep,
By day, at eve, in midnight deep,
Soothed in their flower-dreams soft and sweet
By thy young heart's delicious beat ;
And I shall think of them and thee,
And deeply. long with both to be,
Feeling perchance a sad regret
That I am not a violet.

But of these flowers, dear lady, take
The loveliest one, and, for my sake,

Within the book thou lovest best,
Let its poor, fading leaves be pressed ;
Then keep it through the coming years,
Oft nurtured by thy smiles and tears,
And let it ever, ever be
Love's token-flower from me to thee.

THOUGHTS ON THE FAR PAST.

[WRITTEN AMID THE RUINS OF THE OLD SPANISH MISSION-HOUSE
NEAR SAN ANTONIO, TEXAS.]

A MID these ruins, gloomy, ghostly, strange,
 The weird memorials of an elder time,
The sacred relics of dead centuries,
I stand in utter loneliness ; and thoughts
As solemn as the mysteries of the deep
Come o'er me, like the shadow of a cloud
O'er the still waters of a lonely lake,
Or like the mournful twilight of eclipse
O'er the dim face of Nature.
       Ye were reared,
Oh ruins old, by stern and holy men—
God's messengers unto a new-found world—
Whose voices, like the trumpet of the blast,
Resounded through the forests, and shook down,
As by an earthquake's dread iconoclasm,
The idols that men worshipped.   Their great lives
Were given to awful duty, and their words

Swelled, breathed, and burned and throbbed upon the air
In solemn majesty.   They did not shrink
Or falter in the path of thorn and rock
Their souls marked out.   Their moldered relics lie
Beneath yon humble mounds; but ah, their names,
There rudely sculptured upon blocks of stone,
Are breathed on earth with reverential awe,
And written by God's finger on His scroll
Of saints and martyrs.
                  Age has followed age
To the abysses of Eternity;
And many generations of our race
Have sprung and faded like the forest leaves;
The mightiest temples reared by human pride
Have long been scattered by a thousand storms —
But ye remain.   Ah yes, ye still remain,
And many pilgrims yearly turn aside
From their far journeyings, to come and pause
Amid your shattered wrecks, as lone and wild
As those of Tadmor of the desert.   Wolves
Howl nightly in your ghostly corridors,
And here the deadly serpent makes his home.
Yet round your broken walls, your fallen roofs,
Your many crumbling, shattered images,
Your sunken floors, your shrines with grass o'ergrown,
And the unnumbered strange, mysterious flowers,
That stand, pale nuns, upon your topmost heights,

Wild chants and soul-like dirges seem to rise,
And the low tones of eloquence and prayer
Seem sounding on the hollow winds; and here
I kneel as lowly as I could have knelt,
If I had listened to the living words
Your grand old founders uttered in the name
Of God, who sent them to proclaim His will.

TO LITTLE VIRGILINE GRIFFIN.

YOU are a charming little sprite,
A thing of love and joy and light,
You 're full of sweetness and of grace ;
Sweet is your name, more sweet you face,
So you shall be our baby queen,
Oh, dearest little Virgiline.

You 're sweeter than the sweetest rose
That in the early spring-time blows ;
You 're sweeter than the violet
When its young leaves with dews are wet—
Your very sighs more sweet by half
Than any other baby's laugh ;
Your counterpart was never seen,
Oh, darling little Virgiline.

Should I awake from visions bright,
In the deep silence of the night,
And see a form before me rise,
Like that which gladdens now my eyes,
Oh, I should think it was a fair

And blessed angel of the air,
A being sent down from the skies
To dry my tears, to hush my sighs,
And toward the vision I would lean
With rapture, loveliest Virgiline.

Within the dark depths of your eyes,
As in the blue depths of the skies,
I gaze with ecstasy, and lo !
Bright, wingéd things flit to and fro,
And their rich music-tones are flung
Like bird-notes when the year is young.
Ah, dear one, if you are so good
And beautiful in babyhood,
If you have such bewitching power
Ere your life's bud has burst to flower,
What will you be at sweet sixteen ?—
Canst tell me, baby Virgiline ?

ON THE SUMMIT OF THE SIERRA MADRE.

PERCHED like an eagle on this kingly height,
  That towers toward heaven above all neighboring
    heights,
Owning no mightier but the King of kings,   •
I look abroad on what seems boundless space,
And feel in every nerve and pulsing vein
A deep thrill of my immortality.
How desolate is all around ! No tree,
Or shrub, or blade, or blossom, ever springs
Amid these bald and blackened rocks ; no wing
Save the fell vulture's ever fans the thin
And solemn atmosphere ; no rain e'er falls
From passing clouds—for this stupendous peak
Is lifted far above the summer storm,
Its thunders and its lightnings. As I hold
Strange converse with the Genius of the place,
I feel as if I were a demi-god,
And waves of thought seem beating on my soul
As ocean billows on a rocky shore
O'erstrown with moldering wrecks.

I look abroad,
And to my eyes the whole world seems unrolled
As 't were an open scroll. . The beautiful,
Grand, and majestic, near and far, are blent
Like colors in the bow upon the cloud.
Illimitable plains, with myriad flowers,
White, blue, and crimson, like our country's flag;
The green of ancient forests, like the green
Of the old ocean wrinkled by the winds;
Cities and towns, dim and mysterious,
Like something pictured in the dreams of sleep;
A hundred streams, with all their wealth of isles,
Some bright and clear, and some with gauze-like mists
Half-veiled like beauty's cheek; tall mountain-chains,
Stretching afar to the horizon's verge,
With an intenser blue than that of heaven,
Forever beckoning to the human soul
To fly from pinnacle to pinnnacle
Like an exulting storm-bird: these, all these,
Sink deep into my spirit like a spell
From God's own Spirit, and I can but bow
To Nature's awful majesty, and weep
As if my head were waters.
                         Fare-thee-well,
Old peak, bold monarch of the subject clouds,
That crouch in reverence at thy feet; I go
Afar from thee—to stand where now I stand

Oh, nevermore.   Yet through my few brief years
Of mortal being, these wild wondrous scenes,
On which thou gazest out eternally,
Will be a picture graven on my life,
A portion of my never-dying soul.
What God has pictured Time may not erase.

NEW ENGLAND.

FOR A CELEBRATION IN KENTUCKY OF THE LANDING
OF THE PILGRIMS.

CLIME of the brave! the high heart's home!—
  Laved by the wild and stormy sea!
Thy children, in this far-off land,
    Devote, to-day, their hearts to thee;
Our thoughts, despite of space and time,
To-day are in our native clime,
Where passed our sinless years, and where
Our infant heads first bowed in prayer.

Stern land! we love thy woods and rocks,
    Thy rushing streams, thy winter glooms,
And Memory, like a pilgrim gray,
    Kneels at thy temples and thy tombs:
The thoughts of these, where'er we dwell,
Come o'er us like a holy spell,
A star to light our path of tears,
A rainbow on the sky of years.

Above thy cold and rocky breast
   The tempest sweeps, the night-wind wails,
But Virtue, Peace, and Love, like birds,
   Are nestled 'mid thy hills and vales;
And Glory, o'er each plain and glen,
Walks with thy free and iron men,
And lights her sacred beacon still
On Bennington and Bunker Hill.

ODE ON THE UNVEILING OF THE CLAY STATUE

AT LOUISVILLE, KY., MAY 30, 1867.*

HAIL! true and glorious semblance, hail!
  Of him, the noblest of our race.
We seem, at lifting of thy veil,
  To see again his living face!—
To hear the stirring words once more,
  That like the storm-god's cadence pealed
With mightier power from shore to shore
  Than thunders of the battle-field.

Lo! that calm, high, majestic look,
  That binds our gaze as by a spell—
It is the same that erst-while shook
  The traitors on whose souls it fell!
Oh, that he were again in life!—
  To wave, as once, his wand of power,
And scatter far the storms of strife
  That o'er our country darkly lower!

* Sung at the time by a chorus of one hundred voices.

Again, again, and yet again,
   He rolled back Passion's roaring tide,
When the fierce souls of hostile men
   Each other's wildest wrath defied.
Alas! alas! dark storms at length
   Sweep o'er our half-wrecked Ship of State,
And there seem none with will and strength
   To save her from her awful fate!

But thou, majestic image, thou
   Wilt in thy lofty place abide,
And many a manly heart will bow
   While gazing on a nation's pride;
And, while his hallowed ashes lie
   Afar beneath old Ashland's sod,
One gaze at thee should sanctify
   Our hearts to country and to God.

We look on thee, we look on thee,
   Proud statue, glorious and sublime,
And years, as if by magic, flee—
   And leave us in his grand old time!
Oh, he was born to bless our race
   As ages after ages roll!
We see the image of his face—
   Earth has no image of his soul!

Proud statue! if the nation's life,
  For which he toiled through all his years,
Must vanish in our wicked strife,
  And leave but groans and blood and tears—
If all to anarchy be given,
  And ruin all our land assail,
He'll turn away his eyes in Heaven,
  And o'er thee we will cast thy veil!

ADDRESS

AT THE OPENING OF A NEW THEATER IN LOUISVILLE, KY., MARCH 25, 1867.*

FOR long, long years, all past but not forgot,
A modest temple rose upon this spot,
Devoted to the Drama's noble art—
To give amusement and to touch the heart,
To wield at will with passion's strong control,
To mould the feelings, to exalt the soul,
To kindle thoughts allied to hope and fear,
To wake Joy's smile and holy Pity's tear.
The sinking sun upon that temple shone:
The sun arose—lo! 't was forever gone!
At night's deep moon, when all the circling air
Was gentle as the cadences of prayer,
Where naught was heard above, beneath, around,
Save yonder waterfall's low, solemn sound,
Borne like a tone of mystery and dread

* Recited by Miss Dargon.

Through what might seem a city of the dead—
At that calm hour, beneath the star's sweet ray,
The fell Fire-spirit seized upon his prey;
No help, no mortal help, alas! was nigh—
The flames sprang upward toward the reddened sky;
High in their burning chariots seemed to roam
The Muses, wailing for their perished home;
The clouds above in crimson glory stood,
As if surcharged with awful showers of blood.
But soon the wild and lurid scene was o'er—
The flames sank down, the temple was no more.
But look! upon this spot to memory dear,
What beauty and magnificence appear!—
Up from the blackened ashes, bleak and cold,
A temple rises, nobler than the old;
Heaven guard it well, and may its pride remain
Till hoar antiquity its walls shall stain.

And proudly, now, ye good, and brave, and fair,
We consecrate it to your generous care.
Here, oft will glow the floating dancer's skill;
Here, music sweet your living heart-chords thrill;
Here, histrionic genius' lightning-flame
Awake the thunders of your loud acclaim;
And flowers of beauty spring, forever new—
Your smiles the sunshine, and your tears the dew.

And here, diffusing mirth and tender pain,
The Comic and the Tragic Muse will reign:
Here, poor old Lear, all desolate, will bow
His snow-white hair on dead Cordelia's brow,
And raise his tottering form—weak, worn, and frail—
To dare the rain, the thunder, and the gale;
Here, Shylock, grim, with heart too hard to feel,
Will lift his scales and whet his cruel steel;
Here, Hamlet, gloomy, but with heart of fire,
Avenge the murder of his royal sire;
Here, Richard, in his wild affright, will leap
From the red vision of his horrid sleep,
And see, with wild and frenzied soul and eye,
The ghosts of murdered victims trooping by;
Here, weird Macbeth will vainly seek to clasp
The airy dagger in his desperate grasp,
And his fiend-mate, despairing, strive in vain
From her curst hands to wash the murder-stain;
Here, Juliet, from her balcony, bend low
To see and hear her much-loved Romeo—
Return him tear for tear, and sigh for sigh,
And hail it her last joy with him to die;
Here, girdled Falstaff laugh, with wheezing breath—
Mercutio jest, e'en in the arms of death;
And Rosalind, pure, beautiful, and good,
Thread the dark mazes of the tangled wood.

Aye, we will group within our ample plan,
All fancies of " the myriad-minded man".

If we have done, and still do, well our parts,
Our proud appeal is to your hands and hearts :
We ask your favor ; it will be our task
To render back the worth of all we ask,
And make our new-born Temple's honored name
A portion of your goodly city's fame.

www.ingramcontent.com/pod-product-compliance
Lightning Source LLC
Chambersburg PA
CBHW031954060726
47497CB00016B/2087